8. 10-88

C000165202

The Godwin Sideboard

He was dead.

There were two red-rimmed holes in the check shirt, over his heart, and down the front of it was glistening, sticky-red blood. His body had slid downwards, the legs under the well of his pedestal desk, and one arm thrown out across the top, scattering papers.

He was dead.

Only thirty minutes ago he'd been talking to me on the phone. I couldn't grasp it.

He really was dead.

After the first shock of finding the body of his art-dealer friend, Peter Blackwell, art investment specialist Tim Simpson began asking why Blackwell had been killed. Why had he telephoned on his way back from Sussex to London asking Tim to meet him, edgy rather than jubilant over the find he had just made?

Tim had asked him to look for a sideboard by the Victorian designer E. W. Godwin, sometime lover of actress Ellen Terry, but when Tim followed Peter's trail into Sussex there was no evidence that he had ever unearthed such a piece. Instead there was more violence, an old rugger friend of Tim's, now a police inspector—and Marianne.

Marianne was a partner in Applemore Antiques, San Francisco. Very soon she was Tim Simpson's partner in bed. And in his investigations. And that was when things really hotted up.

JOHN MALCOLM

The Godwin Sideboard

The second Tim Simpson adventure

COLLINS, 8 GRAFTON STREET, LONDON W1

William Collins Sons & Co. Ltd
London · Glasgow · Sydney · Auckland
Toronto · Johannesburg

First published 1984
© John Malcolm 1984

British Library Cataloguing in Publication Data

Malcolm, John
  The Godwin sideboard.—(Crime Club)
  I. Title
  823'.914[F]   PR6063.A36/

  ISBN 0 00 231961 6

Photoset in Linotron Baskerville by
Rowland Phototypesetting Ltd
Bury St Edmunds, Suffolk
Printed in Great Britain by
William Collins Sons & Co. Ltd, Glasgow

CHAPTER 1

She looked like that blonde model that Willie Orpen used to paint. The French or Belgian one that he picked up when he was an official war artist. Orpen had quite an affair with her; it went on into the nineteen-twenties, when he transferred his affections to someone else. Whenever I see Orpen's painting of her—Yvonne, that was her name—sitting on a bed in the morning sunlight, reading a letter with her knees drawn up, in a relaxed pose and totally absorbed, with her coffee untouched beside her, I think of Marianne.

My mind is full of irrelevant details connected with art history and it often associates people and places with such things. Maybe some psychic wave, or latent vibe, planted the idea in my head all unknowingly when I strolled up the Little Boltons that April evening on my way to Peter's shop. The walk takes you past the end of South Bolton Gardens, where Orpen, the most famous and the richest portrait painter of his day, had his studio house. He made his wealthy clients queue outside it in their Rolls-Royces while they waited their turn to be painted.

When Orpen broke up with Evie, as he called her, he gave her his own Rolls-Royce. He was always a generous man. In those days the chauffeur always went with the car, so Orpen passed him on and Evie married him—the chauffeur, I mean—and made a success of it. It's a romantic story and it all took place in France, far away from the studio in South Bolton Gardens, where Orpen drank himself to death at an early age.

Fifty years ago, I thought, as I strolled by. I wasn't born then and Orpen was fifty-three. What would I do if I thought I had only got another twenty years to go? I dismissed the thought; my real preoccupation, at that moment, was with other associations with the area. I had just crossed Cathcart Road, where Ellen Terry's parents once had a house and, ahead of me, beyond the Old Brompton Road, stands Barkston Gardens, home of the famous actress herself for a while. The whole of Earls Court is redolent with Terry family memories because they moved there in a big way when the area was first being changed from market gardens to the terraced maze it has become; long before poor Willie Orpen's time. I'd often chatted about it to Peter because, to reach his shop, you turned right at the Old Brompton Road to the corner of Drayton Gardens, where he was part of the thriving crossroads, with its pub, shops and café. An odd place, in some ways, to have an antique shop, being neither in Chelsea nor Kensington nor Earls Court.

But then Peter Blackwell was hardly an ordinary antique dealer.

His voice on the telephone had been excited. I always thought of Peter as an eternal art student, rather than the highly specialized dealer that he really was, so that his enthusiasms were well known to me. This time, though, the edge on his voice was different; it wasn't just the tension of someone who has stumbled on a real find because there wasn't the jubilance that you get in those circumstances. It was much edgier. The pips cut him off just as I agreed to meet him at his shop. He was out of change and had stopped on the road, in South London somewhere, not even waiting to get back before he rang me, to get me to meet him as soon as he arrived.

If Sue Westerman had still been around I would have got there sooner. But Sue had gone to Australia on a year's exchange with one of the major galleries which her employer, the bloody Tate, mindless of my happiness, had arranged for her. Sue said that she was sorry and would miss me but, with Sue, her career always came first; before Tim Simpson anyway. What I really mean is that I would have been cheesed off with Peter's interruption and would have grabbed a taxi, so as to get it over quickly and be back home with her again. But she wasn't there and there wasn't much else to do, so I decided to walk. After all, it wasn't very far and it was a fine April evening, with a crisp clear sky and the buds sprouting in my part of the Fulham Road. All I had to do was to amble up the Hollywood Road in the fine twilight, cross Cathcart Road, dogleg into the Little Boltons and there I was, with my thoughts and memories roused by the ghosts that glide around those cool, porticoed terraces. It didn't take long.

The lights were on in the window, where Peter had a spotlight on an oak structural reformed Gothic table, with those tremendous arched architectural supports that you get in real Pugin octagonal centre tables. It was sold, of course, because even though that sort of furniture is collected by only a few specialists and museums, Peter was one of the absolute experts in it. Apart from the auction rooms, there are only four or five dealers in London to whom you'd go for that sort of gear.

The door was open, as he said it would be.

Behind the window lights it was difficult to see, because the contrast made the shop dark. I could, however, smile as I saw the gable-roofed outline of a big revolving bookcase in the Bedford Park Queen Anne manner, standing in my way like a great old-fashioned pillar-box with enveloped top and waved Gothic feet. Against the far wall was a vast black sideboard of the Aesthetic Movement, all mirrors and doors and cavities, with holes, crenellations, inlays, handles, balustered shelves and a scooped gallery on top. I winced at it. Who buys that stuff, I thought, God knows, surely even Peter won't be able to sell that.

In the middle of the floor there was a spider centre table surrounded by its own tapering legs and web-like stretchers, all dark and spindly and severe. In the centre of the top stood a vase or vessel, dark red, with whitish erotic figures glazed into it.

'William de Morgan,' I said out loud, picking it up and turning it over so that I could see Peter's label underneath.

Walter Crane. Blast.

Well, I thought, defensively, that dark terracotta red and the white decoration, that's often William de Morgan's line, I'm not so far out. Peter has so many of those sorts of ceramics and they're usually William de Morgan, damn it. So I walked briskly through the rest of the shop, past the chairs and the William Morris settle, the Eastlake sideboard and the long church pew by Butterfield or Street that he'd picked up from a demolished West Country church, to enter his little office at the back, where the desk light was on and he was sitting, slumped sideways, in the oak desk chair of Waterhouse design.

He was dead.

I didn't need to touch him. Peter was a big fellow, my sort of age, with a shock of dark, curly hair and heavy features. He usually wore a woollen tie with a check sports jacket, grey flannels and a check shirt. He had a long, old woollen scarf, a striped one, which he used to wind round and round himself like an undergraduate, scattering ash on to it from the cigarettes he constantly smoked. The scarf was still on, wound round and round his neck, but it hadn't killed him nor had it been of any use in self-defence. He'd been shot.

There were two red-rimmed holes in the check shirt, over his heart, and down the front of it was glistening, sticky-red blood. The impact of the bullets had thrown him back a little, so that his jacket was spread open under the scarf and his head lolled back sideways. His body had slid downwards, with his legs under the well of his pedestal desk, and one arm was still thrown out across the top, scattering papers.

He was dead.

Only thirty minutes or so ago—perhaps forty—he'd been talking to me on the phone. I couldn't grasp it.

He really was dead.

I must have stood there gaping at him for about thirty seconds, completely numb. I took in the office, usually neat, for Peter was methodical, with its filing cabinet and cupboards and typewriter-desk for his secretary and a folio chest. It had all been rifled; there were papers everywhere; the little cash box was open. On his desk, papers were scattered about; old catalogues and photographs were jumbled with invoices, and the bill-spike with its impaled bills lay on its side, so that I could see the last one: a Visa-card receipt from a Hastings garage. When I backed into the shop, away from the office door, I noticed now that the display cabinet where he kept bits of arts and crafts silver and jewellery was open. The shelves were empty. There was no sign of some Ashbee pieces I had looked at a few days back. They were all gone.

The next thing I knew I was on the pavement outside, leaning against a lamp-post and, very soon, I started to vomit, heaving up into the gutter with most of the fry-up I'd made myself for an evening meal. You know how it is when you vomit; it goes all dark and giddy because the blood all leaves your head and goes somewhere else, nearly blacking you out. It wasn't until I was having a breather that vision really returned and I saw the policeman and policewoman standing near me, slightly back and away from me, so as to avoid getting splashed. They had that sort of tolerant, semi-irritated look about them, like you often see on policemen who are dealing with drunks, so I suppose they must have thought that I'd just come out of The Drayton Arms across the road, with a skinful.

At least, that's what I thought; I hoped they didn't think I'd just come out of The Coldharbour, up the road, where all the poofters hang out.

CHAPTER 2

It was in Jeremy's office, overlooking Park Lane, that the fateful idea came to me. We had just finished a review meeting, one of the regular meetings that Jeremy held with his managers to make sure everyone thought they knew what was happening. His office was the biggest in the old, double-fronted Park Lane house and its long French windows opened out on to a balcony. Across the road, opposite, the plane trees in the Park were sprouting and beckoning now, at the end of a wet April morning, to a brighter, crisper place outside.

Jeremy sat back at his big partners' desk and studied the heavily-moulded ceiling which remained from days when the house was the London residence of one of Britain's wealthy, well-connected families. There was a time when the whole of the Lane, fronting on to the Park, was a row of these elegant, wide-eyed buildings of a comfortable domestic scale. Not now; great blocks have been planked down, crushingly, into most of the row; all you have left is the occasional group of houses in terrace form, jumbled together in a compressed fashion between the square slabs.

We had listened to reports of how the market for investment bonds was going; how response to our advertisements was faring; what new 'products' would be coming on the market—by products the managers meant insurance bonds of a different tilt, perhaps property-wards or share-wards—in the near future. It was all going well. Jeremy White's bond-broking office was his own creation, separate, away from the merchant bank that the senior members of his family still ran, but shadowed by it, so that an aura of financial solidity clung to Jeremy's cheerful prospecting for golden seams among the grey stones of personal investment.

He was obviously very bored.

To understand Jeremy you had to comprehend his limit-less desire to preserve money, to keep the taxman's hands off it, not just for himself but for the clientele he had built up and to whom he charged fees, or on whose behalf he invested, keeping a broker's percentage for himself. Brought up amid threatened wealth, like a settler in a besieged stockade, Jeremy's whole being was dedicated to preventing the indi-vidual's precious tin reservoir of liquid funds from seeping away by the corrosion of inflation, from being tapped and siphoned by taxmen or becoming polluted by stagnation. Spend it, yes. Gamble it away by all means. Give it to someone deserving, excellent. But in no circumstances let Government have it by default. That avoidance was Jeremy's inspiration and he threw himself into it, using all his energy, devising new funds, inventing new bonds, sniffing at new tax havens to help his clients and himself to obtain more disposable income from their precious resources.

What did not interest Jeremy was the business of manage-ment or the management of business. The dull, thorough routine of book-keeping, accountability, dimensions, rates, fiscal returns and employment procedures drove him to gloom. For such necessities he employed his managers, hoping quietly that they could be relied upon to do their work thoroughly without telling him too much about it. For this he was prepared to pay generously, but he knew that from time to time he had to be seen to be in charge, to be interested, to be on parade having a word to the troops. It was an honourable sense of duty that his banking family and his years at Eton had instilled into him. One day, perhaps, when his uncle, who ran the Bank, White's Bank in the City of London, accepted him as a responsible member, he might have to make greater call on that sense of duty and get more involved in the routines that bored him. Until then, as long as he was making money as a bond broker and cocking a snook at the stuffy respectability of the Bank, he could keep his involvement to a token one, like our meetings on Mondays.

His eyes swivelled down from the scroll-encrusted ceiling and caught mine. I was picking up my papers, like the rest, preparing to leave him with Geoffrey Price, the accountant I had once, when an outside consultant, picked to run Jeremy's financial affairs for him and who had been partly responsible for my joining the firm.

'Tim!' Jeremy stopped me. 'Don't go! Yes, yes, I know, Geoffrey, we have some important points to cover together but I simply must have a word with Tim while I'm thinking about it.'

He waited until the three of us were alone and then went across to a Chinese lacquer cabinet where the drinks were kept. We had a general rule that it was not to be opened before noon and, glancing at my watch, I realized that it was quarter past. Jeremy, always the gentleman, served us with gin and tonic before he got down to business.

'I was thinking over the weekend,' he said abruptly, 'about the Art Investment Fund.'

He looked at me. Geoffrey took a nervous swig at his glass. The Art Investment Fund was my responsibility, indeed the reason for my joining the firm. Jeremy offered it to me when, in one of his outside-chance, creative-investment moods, he had the idea that his company should set up a fund that invested in art and antiques. It was not a new idea even then, because there were already one or two similar funds, quite apart from British Rail's Pension Fund and Getty, but Jeremy and I had interests in common and he felt that we could do it better. So, at the end of the consulting assignment I was doing for him, I joined him. Mention of the Fund, however, made Geoffrey Price a bit tense. Like most ac-countants, he was not averse to high-risk investments here

and there but Art, well, Art is close to fashion and fashion
has a habit of sudden, unpredictable changes, puncturing
revelations about fakes, and the attentions of con men.
Despite the obvious evidence of financial gain by discriminating collectors and the fall from grace of a casino-like Stock
Exchange, accountants are still biased in favour of traditional investments. Our Art Investment Fund was for speculative money, Geoffrey knew that, and it brought Jeremy a lot
of the publicity he craved, that too, but all the same it was, to
Geoffrey, a trendy sort of thing, which fellow professionals at
the Bank doubtless deplored.

Jeremy loved it. The acquisitions we had so far made in
paintings, silver and other objects had been reasonably
successful. Several of them adorned Jeremy's town house,
carefully insured by well-placed policies on which we, as
brokers, obtained a commission. It was all fitting in very
well. His own taste for interior decoration was traditional,
but good. He liked to be involved in the Fund.

'Furniture,' he said.

I raised my eyebrows.

'Tim, we really should have some decent furniture in the
Fund. No, I don't mean that. We should have some really
exceptional furniture in the Fund, something really first-rate
and rare. No point in going for humdrum run-of-the-mill.
We should set an example. Buy a really cracking piece. Eh?'

In principle, of course, he was right.

'In principle, Jeremy, you are, of course, right,' I said. 'It's
the practice that presents the problems. One may decide, for
example, to go for the finest. What would that be? In
England, a piece by Chippendale? Or, as a second string, by
Hepplewhite, or Vile and Cobb, or Adam, or whatever. Fully
authenticated, of course. Or, you might go for a rare and
early piece. A walnut and gilt bureau-bookcase or a fantastic
marquetry bit or a piece of exceptional carved early oak from
some famous house.'

He looked pleased. 'Well, there you are. Lots of choice, isn't there? All getting rarer, of course, but that's what makes it vital to get in soon.'

I looked at my glass and shook my head gently. 'The problem there, Jeremy,' I said, 'is that everyone else in the trade who's got any money is thinking the same way. You'll have to pay top whack to get the piece, whether it's at auction or from a respectable dealer and you've really gained no advantage over anyone else. Our expertise as fund managers is supposed to be in spotting the investment before everyone else, not with or after them. We have to be better, to make our choice the one that goes up in value more than anyone else's.'

Geoffrey was nodding sagely. Jeremy clapped his hands. 'Bravo! Well said, Tim! Of course we have to. We have to pick the dark horses that—that—'

'Turn up trumps?'

He burst out laughing. 'Yes, yes, turn up a dark horse, very good, mixed metaphors, Tim, you know I love them. Yes, whatever you want to say; end as winners, whatever. We should try to identify pieces which are not so highly prized now but which will go up in value more than the others over the period we advise—usually five years or more for the Fund. Tremendous publicity. So what do you say?'

And that was when the idea came into my mind, an idea born of personal interest and prejudice, like many, but with a conviction I had that anyone who gives advice has to have, or else keep his mouth shut. Later, I might think it was all to do with London's vibes again because, at that moment, looking out of the long windows at the sprouting trees across the way, my eye caught sight of a park-keepers' hut, a black-panelled one, with a deep-eaved roof and diagonal planking, on short stilts, which gave it a vaguely Oriental look, almost like a Japanese temple.

'We should buy,' I said casually, like Pandora opening her fateful box on the calm beach, 'a sideboard by E. W. Godwin.'

CHAPTER 3

'Twenty-five thousand?' queried Geoffrey incredulously. 'For that? Are you sure?'

Jeremy scowled at him.

The furniture department of the Victoria and Albert Museum starts on the lower floors at the fifteenth or six-teenth century and works its way upwards to the twentieth. We had ascended the marble-streaked flights of stairs to the top and were half way along the galleries, well into the eighteen-sixties. The partitioned side-area we were looking at had several pieces by Godwin in it, including occasional tables, chairs and an oak writing cabinet.

What was engaging our attention particularly, however, was an odd black Japanese-looking piece composed of four black-panelled boxes connected by a simplified Oriental system of square-sectioned supports and legs that left spaces in between. There were open shelves and drawers; silver hinges and handles; odd little black square rails, one of them intended as a plate rack, traversed the spaces. Each box was, in fact, a cabinet with a panelled door, and the doors had leather paper inset into the panels, which emphasized the shiny black lacquering of the other surfaces. Space and mass, the preoccupation of all architects, was what dictated the design of the piece. On the outside edges hung two black flaps, which could be put up and supported by a hinged bracket, like a Pembroke table. Put this way, the thing sounds fussy, but actually it was all very simple and, like all simple designs, was very sophisticated.

Geoffrey Price cleared his throat. The atmosphere at the Victoria and Albert had induced in him, to start with, a certain deference, even a reverence, for the objects it contained. Geoffrey, after all, as an accountant, had great respect for the established structure of society and its officially recognized values. Now he seemed hesitant.

'Tim,' he quavered, 'I—um—I know that you're really the expert in this field, but are you sure, I mean, isn't there a risk—?'

I smiled at him. I've always liked Geoffrey. 'The last one of these to appear at auction was at Sotheby's and it went for twenty-five thousand pounds. I swear to you. It's a matter of record. You know me; I've got every record that can be kept on art investment.'

He hastened to make restitution. 'I'm sure, Tim, I'm sure. But was it—perhaps—a flash in the pan?'

I shook my head. 'There are quite a few museums, not to mention a few collectors, who are after one of these. It's not, as you can see, the workmanship or the craftsmanship particularly that you're buying, it's the design. No, actually, it's Art. This piece qualifies as a work of art rather than a piece of furniture, mainly because it's a milestone in the history of design. You can see that it's not far from this, made in the eighteen-sixties or seventies, to the Modern Movement. A chunk of design history. Much the same argument applies to Mackintosh furniture and look what those buggers up in Glasgow are willing to pay for that.'

'Ninety-odd thousand,' murmured Jeremy, nodding. He leant across the restraining cords and tapped the side of the piece with a cautious finger. An attendant looked up sharply.

'It seems,' he muttered, 'a bit—fragile. Are there many about?'

'No, not many. Which is good for investment. There must be more, though. There's one in the Bristol City Museum. It's a little bit different from this and it has a Japanese watercolour let into the top door panels instead of the leather paper. It was probably the prototype and was Godwin's own. He came from Bristol but he designed it while he was living with Ellen Terry. Which should interest you, Jeremy, being a theatrical man.'

His head swung round to me with a quick grin. 'I remember something about that. Didn't he pinch her from the painter, G. F. Watts?'

Geoffrey Price clicked his tongue disapprovingly. 'Watts? He was a famous Academician, surely? I've seen things of his here at the V and A and at Queen Victoria's house on the Isle of Wight. There's even a statue of him right outside. He was a pillar of—'

'Victorian society,' I finished for him drily. 'He was also a bloody old fool. He was forty-eight when he married Ellen Terry and she was sixteen. What do you say of a society which vastly values respectability but stands solemnly by at a wedding where a raw girl of sixteen is married to a neurotic bachelor three times her age? The nuptial night was a disaster. He continued to live at Little Holland House, in a household dominated and run for him by a married middle-aged woman friend, Mrs Prinsep, who never gave Ellen Terry, as a new wife, the slightest chance to establish herself. It wasn't surprising that she went off with Godwin, whom she knew from Bristol days, and whose first wife had died.'

Jeremy wasn't listening. He was standing back, looking at the sideboard. He might have been something of a traditionalist, but he was keen on interior design. No interior designer of modern imagination could reject a Godwin sideboard. Jeremy was intrigued, which meant that the boredom of the morning had left him. In Jeremy's veins ran the blood of an ancestor who had traded in South American timber and who would have regarded banking as a safe, supine activity, devoid of stimulating risks.

'Twenty-five thousand,' he murmured. 'Not a lot really,

for a work of art. Not internationally.'

I raised a warning finger. 'The international aspect is not altogether clear, Jeremy,' I said. 'The Commonwealth, yes. Some American collectors and museums without a doubt. I don't see the Continentals going for this too much, though.'

He nodded, understanding, but posed a question I'd been waiting for.

'This is Aesthetic Movement stuff, isn't it? I thought you once said that Aesthetic Movement pieces aren't popular?'

I nodded. 'Correct. Godwin was a leader of the Aesthetic Movement. A friend of Burges, Whistler and Oscar Wilde. Wilde even wrote sonnets to Ellen Terry while she was living with Godwin. But this furniture, this Anglo-Japanese stuff, was copied about all over the place. You mustn't confuse the commercial copies and the fussy derivative stuff with the real McCoy. Authenticated pieces by famous architects or designers are quite apart from the rest.'

Jeremy shoved his hands in his pockets and cocked his head to one side, so that his blond hair gleamed sharply as he made the movement. He was a big man, still reasonably well-shaped for one with a clear love of rich diet and a tendency to run to fat, but still striding through his early forties with energy and bravura, as they say in painting circles. In the dusty light of the Victoria and Albert Museum, filtered by the linen blinds on the big windows and spangled dully through four small stained-glass windows of Arthurian legendary scenes which I guessed to be Burne-Jones and Morris's work, he stood freshly laundered, stripe-suited and polished in a way that made the subfusc furnishings look jaded. Only the Godwin sideboard, shining black with bright silver trappings, made an exotic Eastern challenge to his well-tailored surfaces. The blond patrician figure glanced around him, across the aisle, where a selection of Morris and Webb furniture, including the vast Gothic cabinet made by Seddon, the mock-medieval oak refectory table of Webb's and an adjustable bobbin-turned easy chair with dull, safe 'Bird' tapestry upholstery stood glumly by. His gaze swept across this once-trendy ensemble, taking in the self-conscious decoration and the unyielding, spindly, rush-seated Sussex country chairs, precursors of decades of Hampstead intellectual discomfort, dotted within it. He grimaced.

'My God,' he said in his richest Park Lane tones, 'that William Morris stuff is appallingly middle-class. Don't you think so, Tim?'

Geoffrey Price gave a nervous start and glanced about him, to see if anyone had heard. It was not that Geoffrey was a great fan of William Morris; after all, he had been one of the most famous Socialists and therefore not One Of Us, so to speak, but, well, after all, he was now part of British history and one had to be careful . . .

His discomfiture amused me. I was inclined to agree with Jeremy. Beside the Morris section, the Godwin piece looked positively racy, rakish and low-slung, with its flaps out to give length to its proportion. It might not have conformed to traditional cabinetwork principles and it was distinctly odd, but at least it had originality, even if based on some Japanese precedent, far away.

Jeremy turned back to it. 'Godwin,' he murmured, 'Godwin. I say, Tim, there's no connection with that painter lady, that Sickert woman, Mary Godwin, that you had that little—er—imbroglio about, involving my cousin, is there?'

Jeremy had a memory like an elephant.

'The painter of *A Back Room in Somers Town*, you mean. I don't think so; different generations, anyway. But it's possible. Mary Godwin came from Bristol, too. Could have been related, I suppose. Never thought of it.'

He smiled at me, benignly. 'Just that I wouldn't like to think that this might lead to—should we say—another involvement, Tim?'

I sighed wearily. 'No, Jeremy. No involvement. This is just another investment decision.'

Geoffrey stood aside from us, apart, watching in perplexed fashion as Jeremy's eyes roamed once more over the ebony shine and the sharp silver fittings. It all depended on Jeremy now.

He grinned, suddenly. His eyes sparkled.

'All right, Tim,' he said. 'Go on. Be a devil. Buy us one.'

It seemed so easy. All I had to do, when I left them outside the museum, was to jump on a passing bus, the No. 30, Hackney Wick to Putney. It passes Park Lane, then the Victoria and Albert, before turning into the Old Brompton Road, passing the crossroads at Drayton Gardens as it heads westwards, towards the river.

CHAPTER 4

'Good grief,' Peter Blackwell said, puffing on a cigarette, 'this is a turn-up for the book.'

I rested my bottom on the surface of an oak table of ecclesiastical character and smiled at him. Peter was happy. Some carrier's men had just delivered a settle by William Morris which Peter had bought at a faraway auction and we spent a bit of time admiring the spiky floral marquetry let into its surfaces by George Jack, the Morris furniture man, before I told Peter the news. I should explain that William Morris never made any furniture himself, nor was he interested in it; he left it to Philip Webb and George Jack to get on with, being much too preoccupied with wallpaper and fabrics and Icelandic sagas and Socialism and his frustrated wife's affairs with Rossetti to bother about such mundane things as furniture. The settle had left Peter temporarily a few thousand pounds lighter in pocket, but he had sold it, on the telephone, that morning, for several thousand more. Art may be Art, but a dealer has to live.

'A Godwin sideboard,' he said cheerfully, exhaling more smoke. '*Et tu, Brute?* the Jeremy White Fund? Good grief, I say again, a turn-up for the book.'

'Why, have you got one?'

He shook his shaggy head. 'Of course not. But it will be nice to add you to the list.'

I shifted my behind. 'Now come on, Peter, that doesn't sound very ethical. If you are already acting for someone else——?'

He cocked two fingers at me in rude salute.

'Balls. I've given up acting for museums at auction. If I get a cheap price they pay me a fixed percentage and it doesn't even pay for the petrol. So I buy and sell myself; take it or leave it——I'm a dealer now, not a public benefactor. And I have got a standing order for a Godwin sideboard, if I can find one. From more than one of the bastards. Museums, I mean.'

He lit another cigarette and squinted at me, challenging. Peter could be a bit daunting on his home ground. It wasn't just that he was a big man, confident, relaxed in the private knowledge that kept him in front of the pack. It was his additional network of contacts, rich collectors, museum experts, obscure historians and rascally junk dealers that provided several dimensions to his quick grasp of research and his surprisingly cunning intuition where trade secrets were concerned. I recognized that we'd be in for a subtle Dutch auction if Peter got his hands on a Godwin piece, so I said wryly:

'Have they got to have a sideboard? Couldn't you sell them another piece, like a bureau or something?'

He shook his head dubiously. 'Doubt it. It's the sideboard they're all after. The other pieces do fetch a bit, but the sideboard is the design that you can identify as a step on the road to the Modern Movement. It gets all the publicity. You see, Godwin did all sorts of other things, even wallpaper designs, and Gothic things, to keep in fashion, as well as that oak stuff for Dromore Castle in Northern Ireland and the chairs that everyone copied. There's one over there.'

He gestured towards a corner, scattering ash on to his tweed jacket. The chair he indicated had a circular seat, splayed legs and a barred, open back, half-circular, with a thick top rail.

'Is that a real one?'

He grinned at me. 'Suspicious bugger. Yes, it is, but I know what you mean. After the William Watt catalogue was published in eighteen-seventy-seven, with all those Godwin designs in it, a lot of greedy commercial men copied that chair. There is a way of identifying the copies from the originals, though.'

'How?'

He tapped the side of his nose. 'That's my business. You make your money your way, I'll make it mine.'

I liked Peter. I had been dropping in on him for a chat for some years, long before I joined Jeremy White, when my ex-wife Carol had first got me trailing round antique markets. She didn't like Peter or the period and designs that inspired him, but I did. After the divorce, I felt no hesitation in seeing him. There were lots of other dealers I knew, nearly all of them much more traditional in their taste and serving a much bigger market, but none of them had Peter's ability to break new ground or research their period as thoroughly as he did. There was none of your average-brown-mahogany-type dealer about Peter Blackwell.

I decided to draw him out a bit further.

'Look,' I said, 'the Bristol sideboard was made around, say, eighteen-sixty-seven, when Godwin called it a "black buffet" in his drawing-room, presumably in London, or perhaps Harpenden, where he set up house with Ellen Terry. The Victoria and Albert one is eighteen-seventy-six; they know that because the leather paper in the top and other panels wasn't imported until that year from Japan by Liberty's. Just one year later, in eighteen-seventy-seven, Godwin sells his designs to a commercial man, William Watt, who produces a catalogue called Art Furniture—very trendy—that was such a sell-out that it had to be reprinted. Right?'

Peter smirked tolerantly through his cigarette-smoke. 'Right so far, Tim. All a matter of record but ten out of ten for effort. Ask me another.'

'I will. How many of these bloody sideboards were made, then? How many between eighteen-sixty-seven and eighteen-seventy-six firstly; and how many as a result of Watt's catalogue of eighteen-seventy-seven which was such a rave success?'

He shook his head gently. 'No idea. No one knows.'

There are times when the sheer bloody obtuseness of the antique trade drives me to distraction. Peter was one of the most well-informed about his own particular period but I suppose that he was too busy making a living to be able to spend time on original research into this sort of thing. It's often left to women historians who can be supported by loving husbands while they spend the days digging up cross-references and unearthing obscure invoices that prove some vitally important dates. The odd thing is that men like Peter and other dealers despise those sorts of women and their published work outwardly, but they use it to confirm their own quietly-obtained vital facts, which they produce like trump cards when the moment to make money arrives. You can't blame them; if your next bottle of plonk depended on your keeping your mouth shut, you'd put a padlock on it and not shoot it off to show how clever you are, like the stupid ones do.

I kept cool and asked him: 'Well, how many have come to light?'

'Oh, apart from the two you've covered, about three more; maybe four. One at Sotheby's. One elsewhere. One quite recently, bought by an Australian museum from the States. I have a collector client—and I'm not going to give you his name—who has one here in his house in London. He bought it a few years back at a Surrey auction, for an absolute song.'

'The States? You mean there may be some in the States?'

He shrugged. 'Why not? A piece by Burges turned up recently in Detroit and he was a pal of Godwin's. After all, it's quite possible that there may be several. Think of all those so-called blasted antique dealers who have sent thousands of containerloads of furniture to America, most of it Victorian or Edwardian, or even repro. They haven't the faintest idea what they're handling half the time. And remember, Eastlake furniture was very popular in America in the eighteen-sixties and seventies, so why not Godwin? Who knows what Watts sold? Think of the publicity—Ellen Terry was very popular, a great favourite over there.'

'Oh, come on, Peter, that was much later, and even American Victorian morality would have kept things quiet in that direction.'

He shrugged again. To Peter, the Ellen Terry connection was quite irrelevant. She was just a side-issue, a bit of spicy journalistic gossip fringing on a serious subject. In Peter's desk there were original photographs of Burges's Tower House in London and reams of useful design information that helped him to identify and corroborate pieces that he surreptitiously examined at auction. The amorous and matrimonial affairs of these key figures were of little value in making money unless they helped him to establish a date, an owner, a succession leading to a provenance. His mind was starting to wander.

'Did he give Ellen Terry any of his own furniture?'

He frowned. 'The daughter—Edith Craig—she had some.
That's at Bristol.'

'Did he have it when they ran off together?'

'Christ knows. She was so fed up with those women—what
was their name—I've forgotten—they all married well—
Mrs Prinsep at Holland House and her sister the famous
photographer, Julia Cameron, her snaps sell for a bit nowadays, and the other sister, Lady Somers—'

'Somers?'

'Yes, why?'

'Nothing.'

'Well, anyway, I think she just ran off and took anything
that Godwin offered. He was quite a lady's man, you know.'

'Really?'

'Died early. Only fifty-three.'

'Like Willie Orpen.'

'Who?'

The conversation was getting out of control. I often find
that once you start these past-times reminiscences and ex-
changes, the whole thing gets terribly out of hand. If Peter
and I went on this way the cross-references would never
cease and we would get hopelessly enmeshed in fascinating
but otherwise useless pieces of historical information.

'There might be something left at Small Hythe, but I
doubt it. Godwin's not terribly popular with the Ellen Terry
buffs because he left her to marry Miss Philip.'

'So did Sir Henry Irving leave her for another but they
don't seem to execrate him.'

'Ah, but he was theatrical. An actor. People always forgive
actors.'

At that moment we were interrupted by Peter's secretary,
Myra, coming in with a sheaf of photographs. Peter had a
succession of secretaries, all of whom he kept at a distance
and all of whom got very possessive about him, whether or
not they wound up with him in the flat upstairs over the shop

for a while. Myra was no exception. I suspected that she was moving in for what she thought of as the kill and that he, tolerantly, would allow her to move into his flat as he had several of his previous secretaries, to share his untidy domesticity for a brief period until she would leave, irritably, like all the others. Peter was not inclined to be pinned down and his whereabouts, as he pursued the elusive artefacts he sought, were never consistently known to anyone, not even a conjugal partner. It was his living and his eccentric way of life, carefully and consistently preserved, in and out of a whole series of shops and auction rooms and pubs from one end of the country to the other, that were at stake. Women, eventually, found his elusive character and habits intolerable. They always left, some sooner than later. Myra would soon find out.

She gave me, now, a sharp glance, as she often did to friends of Peter's who took up his time with speculatively historical conversations. She broke up our chat with a demand for clarification of a sheaf of invoices, photographs and copy for a catalogue. Sighing wearily, he followed her obediently into the little office to deal with them and I excused myself and left. I have often wondered if poor Myra obtained consummation of the relationship she was so obviously aiming to establish before I found Peter, that dreadful evening, after he rang me. But of course I've never dared to ask.

CHAPTER 5

As any other ex-rugger man will tell you, you usually feel a lot better the morning after a good vomit. The purge of the digestive system and the ejection of the potentially toxic material helps to create an optimistic feeling, as though you were making a fresh start.

Not in my case, the next morning.

The noises from the Fulham Road were so insistent that eventually I couldn't ignore them any more and had to admit, even to myself, that I was fully awake and didn't want to be. The enormity of Peter's death made the familiar dog-eared bedroom, the bathroom and the kitchenette where I brewed some tea, seem distant, detached, as though I was looking at them from a new, disillusioned viewpoint. The objects that Peter loved and which I found so fascinating had killed him. The stupidity of the event and the triviality of value that the items missing from his shop would realize sickened me. There was no accepting it. Some other explanation had to be found. I looked vaguely round the flat, searching for something to give me a clue; no Sue Westerman was there to talk to, with her plain, rather priggish, sensible-shoed English common sense.

I missed her. Her absence was like a missing filling to a big tooth. Sue had been living with me for just six months when the offer of the Australian exchange came up. It had seemed to be barely the day before that she moved in from Hampstead, leaving her girlfriends behind and joking that the Fulham Road was a lot nearer Millbank and her job at the Tate Gallery. Thanks for the compliment, I used to say to her, a lad likes to feel needed in some way. Then this bloody Aussie thing came out of the blue; it was the chance of a lifetime and all that crap that they tell you when you first start work and they want to send you somewhere that no one else wants to go.

But Sue wanted to go, damn it.

Whether it was because she felt that the commitment to me had become too close, too binding, too early in life, or whether I was simply turning out to be unsuitable, she never said. We were having a lot of fun, arguing about art happily, without rancour, visiting galleries and the auction rooms together, taking sides about commerce and culture—I was always commerce, she was always culture—eating out a lot, going to parties in Hampstead where her old buddies and Geoffrey Price, through whom I'd met her, still lived. It was an idyllic time, hourless, without any sense of routine, habit, deadlines or the daily grind, even though both of us had our jobs and must have kept to some sort of schedule, however unimportant it may have seemed.

Then, one evening, quite suddenly, she came in and said that she'd been offered this exchange with an Australian gallery and she thought she'd better go because there might never be another chance.

I laughed at first and said what crap you can always go to Aussie, I mean it's all right, I've been there, but once you've eaten the oysters and been on the ferry to Manly and avoided the sharks while you're swimming, there's nothing you can't do inside two weeks. As for culture, for Christ's sake, Sue, you've seen the Sidney Nolans here, and Barry Mackenzie should surely have—

She said, I know, I believe you, but you've seen it and I haven't, I might never get the chance and it's a good step for me and I might not be able to do it some other time, I might have responsibilities, God knows, a family, I have to go.

I said, Sue, don't go.

She said it was only for a year.

Only for a year. Christ.

We didn't get on very well after that. I mean, it was impossible, wasn't it? I saw her off at the airport thinking: *to put the world between us we parted, stiff and dry. Goodbye said you, forget me; I will, no fear, said I.* Some chance. Then I had rather a lot to drink. No, I wasn't going to be frightfully good and understanding about it; perhaps that's why she left nothing behind.

So there I was. Am.

The policeman and policewoman who watched me vomiting on the pavement's edge were plain disbelieving when I got my breath back and told them what it was all about. The policewoman watched me warily while the man went inside the shop, as though it was a trap or a hoax. Then the bloke came out and they moved with commendable speed. Cars arrived with men in raincoats and then photographers. They sat me down solicitously on a chair in the shop—by Frank Brangwyn it was, and worth about two thousand quid or so—and they took my fingerprints after a while, explaining courteously that this was to eliminate my prints from those of others that they might find. Just as courteously they asked me to empty my pockets, which I thought was a bit off, but I was still too upset to argue. I told them my story and the timing several times, to several different blokes. After a while they took me to South Kensington Police Station and spent an interminable time taking a statement from me and checking it and typing it and getting me to sign it. Gradually they started to talk to me, to respond to my queries instead of avoiding them. They were impersonal, detached, as men who have busy professional problems to solve often are, working in their own way like a garage mechanic who ignores your well-informed questions about your car's breakdown and sticks to his own well-tried routines.

It became clear that they believed that Peter had been killed by a thief, entering by coincidence or arrangement through the door left open for me, or maybe even loitering outside, waiting his chance. I said that was bloody ridiculous. The kind of things Peter had in his shop were specialist, unusual, not common antique taste, and difficult to sell for real money in the general market for stolen goods, where conventional silver and jewellery are the desirable items.

The police did not seem to follow the same train of thought. One of their valuers, admittedly, showed a surprised unconcern for the things that I thought were missing, clearly not rating them as of any importance. The general attitude was that some thieves would try anything on the off-chance and that any antique shop was fair game. They did agree that murder, with a gun, was unusual in London, though a surprised thief was often desperate; they were always warning the public about that, not to have a go.

'Peter was sitting down,' I said, 'not having a go.'

You don't know, they said, big fellow wasn't he, probably frightened the wits out of the bloke when he saw him, might have started to get up, position in the chair makes that possible.

'The thief could have run away. The coast behind him was clear. There was no call to shoot, it's utterly inconsistent with normal burglar behaviour, you must know that.'

Look, sir, they said, patiently, here's a bloke with a shooter goes into a shop all tensed up, no other motive but theft as far as we know, now, nerves screaming, and suddenly there's this big fellow glaring at him from the office alcove and he's thinking he's caught or maybe recognized so bang, that's it. Violent crime has been on the increase for several years and you must have read how stupid and petty and unprofitable some, indeed many, of these crimes have been. And what kind of mad, inexperienced tearaways are getting into it, you'd be amazed, let me assure you. The real problem is controlling these guns. We'll keep an open mind, of course we will, but all we can do is to go on the facts pure and simple, and we'll keep in touch.

'What about the 'phone call to me?'

'We'll try and investigate it, see if we can find where he made it from and if there's any relevance, but it will probably be difficult. After all, you can't help us much, can you, sir, you've no idea why he called; could have been anything, any reason. There's nothing in his pockets or his papers to suggest he'd made an important find and he could have been anywhere between Hastings and London, that's half of

South-East England, during the day, but we'll try, believe us, we'll try. So do now go home and let us know if you think of anything else, but leave us to it and thank you very much for your assistance with our inquiries, you've been most helpful, the boys'll run you home, you've had a shock and it's the least we can do.'

My tea went cold while I thought about it. All night long, between fitful dozes, I had thought about it. The only reason Peter would have interrupted the evening so urgently would be if he'd made a find. Antique dealers are careless of nine-to-five timing but they have to have some tangible reason for working late, not just a desire for a chat.

He hadn't said that he'd found something. There wasn't that note in his voice, either. Yet the only thing that connected him with me from a business point of view, right then, was a Godwin sideboard. Had he perhaps heard of one somewhere, found where one was available, or found where one was unavailable, difficult to purchase, that needed some sort of joint strategy to winkle out? That might have been it; perhaps he needed White's to help him; perhaps it was too expensive for him and he would have passed it on to us in return for a commission.

No; it would have to be hellishly expensive for Peter to do that, after what he'd said to me. It wasn't like him. And why meet him at the shop? He knew where I lived, not far away. For a commission deal he could simply have called on me and cadged a free whisky while he talked about it.

Endless, useless speculation. I made some fresh tea, got dressed and rang the office, asking for Jeremy. He wasn't there. Jeremy's office hours were often erratic, but not because he was idle. He might just as well be in the City or wrangling with some other brokers or even with an insurance company itself. His secretary, Penny, said she was expecting him in after lunch and I decided not to explain too much to her. I rang Peter's shop instead.

Myra answered. She was grief-stricken but calm, calm enough at any rate to make her hostility to me quite evident but calm enough to listen carefully to what I wanted, to go down to the office and come back with the information impaled on the bill-spike I had seen overturned but, now, uprighted on Peter's desk. The police were still sifting through the shop and she was staving off imminent collapse by helping them, keeping herself occupied. Poor Myra; perhaps she would realize, one day, that Peter's self-sufficiency had been impregnable, but at least she would have preferred to find that out for herself.

After shaving, I made some instant porridge to line the acid coating of my stomach, ate it, and went out to a nearby kerb where the Volvo estate was parked. Fuel injection is very useful on damp, cough-laden London mornings; I was away towards the river and the South-East very quickly. There was no point in sitting about doing nothing, I couldn't work, and there was one thought in my mind that only personal observation would satisfy.

CHAPTER 6

The road from London to Hastings is a bad one. You think, when you've extricated yourself, raging, from the tangle of shabby South-East London, from Peckham or Lee Green or Lewisham, that all will be plain sailing. You hit the Sevenoaks by-pass, sweep past Tonbridge and imagine that the dual carriageway will last forever. No chance; it funnels into the village of Pembury and winds its picturesque way as a two-lane, much-excavated, converted country track with roadworks or heavy lorries delaying you every ten miles. If William the Conqueror landed now he'd think that they'd constructed the whole thing with the idea of stopping him reaching the Thames. I was in a bad temper by the time I arrived.

As for Hastings, well, anyone who knows Hastings will tell you its problem; it's at the arse end of England. There's no rugby team, the cricket's atrocious and no one has any money. You come into the town under a metal tubular railway bridge that looks as though it's been borrowed from Barnes and you see the tiers of dilapidated houses stretching in ranks up the hill in front of you. Hastings in an exercise in collapsing terraces, fly-blown arcades and littered prom-enades; a haven for the cockle-and-winkle trade, where the families in rusty Marinas visit for fish and chips with a day's amusement at three quid a head. No one successful goes to Hastings except to shake his head at the cheerful failure of a once-thriving resort.

But Peter Blackwell had. The bill on the spike said so.

I eased the Volvo carefully down Queen's Road and passed the garage where Peter had bought his petrol. You couldn't stop; to rub in the success of the town the council have put double yellow lines along most of the streets so as to channel you to the parking areas, like bomb sites, that disfigure some prominent positions. I checked the garage over as I passed but there was nothing to stop for, anyway; it was just a standard self-service filling station making a gap in a dentured old terrace of houses and discount shops. There was a junk dealer's nearby, spilling rubbish and cartons of books on to the pavement, but Peter hadn't been there; I was almost certain where he'd gone.

During the time when antique shops mushroomed in the quaint medieval Old Town of Hastings, to the east of the central mess, Peter had a share in a shop there; I remem-bered him telling me about it. It had been closed for three or four years, since the Continental trade stopped calling and by-passed the town on their route from Folkestone and Dover via Sandgate to Brighton. Peter had no stake in

Hastings any more, but his contacts were good. Hastings was a town that thrived in the late 1870s and '80s, when the booming hop trade of Kent and Sussex swelled the fashion for seaside holidays and the hop pickers, flush with money, headed for the sea. It was always down-market, cheap and cheerful, made for the cockle trade and socially unpretentious. By 1916 it was all over; they left the hops to rot in the fields that year and the population has not grown in numbers since then. When Willie Orpen's brother-in-law, Jack Knewstub, went bankrupt in 1926, he was abandoned by his family and wound up in Hastings with a kettle and a canary for company, as though Hastings was naturally the place for the destitute to head for. Back in that late nineteenth-century boom, however, there were houses in Hastings and in neighbouring St Leonards that were of solid grandeur and mistaken money, fashionably furnished in the latest mode, from Aesthetic Movement to Arts and Crafts. Peter had picked up some very interesting gear around Hastings, without anyone knowing what it was, not even Belgy Klooster on the seafront.

The April wind was pushing the choppy grey water of the Channel into froth as it scudded along the shingled beach, whipping the rusted stanchions of the big old pier. I felt the Volvo rock slightly as a gust caught it, pushing the car away from the iron posts and rails along the wet promenade as I turned westwards. Before the gap-toothed splendour of Warrior Square, before the seedy seafront boarding-houses could claim to be in St Leonards, I saw the cluster of shops and veered across the road, drawing in to the kerb to park behind one of two Luton vans at the pavement. Both were shabby and someone had patched them with metal sheets of a different colour from the original coachwork. The front one, with a blue square adorning a rusty back corner, revved up and pulled away as I walked into the shop.

I got a surprise.

She was standing half way inside, along the rows and tiers of shipping trade goods, stacked one on top of the other in the cavernous interior. Her hand rested on the back rail of one of a set of Korean Chippendale chairs, the sort of repros they make out in Seoul in a livid red shiny hardwood, like raw mahogany that is bleeding to death. It was a long set—by that I mean there were a lot of them—stacked in pairs, the design copied from some Victorian version of an eighteenth-century Chippendale, Gothic in origin, with square legs chamfered on the inside and a drop-in type of seat. The girl was blonde, fair-skinned, in a tailored blouse and skirt. I guessed she was American from her clean, tidy appearance and the bland, almost talcum-dusted finish to her. She had a cracking figure, though; small waist, good bust and, when she turned, her behind pressed firmly against the back of the tailored blue skirt. She glanced back at me, smiled briefly, and then turned to her companion, a slightish bloke in a suit made of pale blue jeans material. I hate jeans suits; the buggers who wear them are all suspect to me. He wore high-heeled cowboy boots to jack himself up and the white shirt under his jean jacket was open wide to reveal the regulation bead necklace on his sunburnt chest. As they moved further into the shop I remember thinking what a waste of a smashing bird.

Belgy came rushing up to me.

'Mr Simpson! Tim! What a surprise! Haven't seen you for now, let me see, ages. Eh?'

Belgy Klooster was stocky, broad and strong of hand-shake. The thick fair skin on his Flemish face looked unlined and yellow, like a Gouda cheese. He was overweight, like many men who work hard physically, because their tiredness makes them overcompensate on beer and chips. Belgy was in the furniture removal business but he would not have called it that, of course. He would have said that he was an antique dealer. Belgy's business was in the furniture shipping trade;

second-hand wardrobes, washstands, desks, chairs, big cupboards, tables, early plywood sideboards. There was nothing
he wouldn't handle if he could stick more than a fiver on it,
but it was heavy trade, unsuitable for weaklings. God knows
what errant wind had blown Belgy on to the pebbled
Hastings strand. Rumour had it that the tax authorities in
his native Antwerp were anxious to talk to him. Another
rumour mentioned drugs and odd duty-free goods that
travelled in his Lutons and his big pantechnicon between
Dover or Newhaven and the Continent. Others said that
Belgy and his boys had given an entirely new meaning to the
phrase 'houses cleared for cash'. Someone told me once that
the furniture and bric-à-brac he brought over as return loads
from Germany and Holland were stuffed full of pornographic
literature and nasty videos, but no one really knew. All they
could see was Belgy and the two strapping tattooed lads he
employed grunting as they heaved the big, unpleasant furniture into the vans. If ever a man lived by the sweat of his
brow, the petrol engine and the wad of banknotes in his back
pocket, it was Belgy Klooster.

He was overdoing the welcome. Dealers like Belgy are very
friendly to people who buy, not to casual callers who waste
their time. I had never been much of a buyer of Belgy's gear,
which was always well picked-over by the professionals,
including Peter. I dropped in now and then, when travels
permitted, because big warehouses like Belgy's fascinate me.
You never know what may turn up. There's something about
the sight of huge quantities of old furniture of varied design
that excites me, like a Jack Russell seeing a huge number of
rabbit holes and sniffing for occupancy, tail awag.

Belgy was usually civil to me because he knew that I was a
friend of Peter's and of several other dealers who bought from
him regularly. From their remarks, he'd soon cottoned on
that I was up the pecking order, somewhere. Not a dealer,
like them, not a punter, but a semi-expert, an Art Fund man,

to be sneered about in private but respected in public, just in case. He had always tolerated my poking about with cool disregard until one day, when they were struggling a bit, I helped to up-end a satinwood Broadwood grand piano with them and stuck it in the Luton. He was a bit warmer after that, treating me not quite so much as the pin-striped wanker he'd obviously thought me to be.

Friendship, however, was another matter. The broad smile and solicitous attention, the pretence of old acquaintance, was new and out of place. Indeed, the broad smile stretched the tight fat face into a rigid mask and the eyes, fixed into folded slits, studied my face with unblinking bonhomie.

'You must be a good customer.' The blue-jeaned suit spoke with that high, Anglicized twang that cultural, intellectual West Coasters affect. 'Belgy's never greeted me that way and look how much I buy.'

He was across the shop, separated from me by a line of Edwardian satin walnut dressing chests with those grooved lines incised horizontally to decorate the drawer fronts. I became aware that a number of yellow stickers adhered to quite a lot of the pieces and, shifting my gaze to one nearby, read the black printed title 'Applemore Antiques, San Francisco'. It is common practice for export buyers to label their purchases this way so that their shippers know what to pick up. The labelled piece my gaze had caught was a 1930s reproduction Jacobethan oak desk with machined mouldings, on a nasty, bulbous, mock-Tudor stand. Dreadful, it was.

He caught my stare and shrugged apologetically.

'Don't you like it? It's my living, you know.'

'Well,' I said slowly, searching for words, 'it's not exactly Jackson Square, is it?'

His face lit up with pleasure. 'You know 'Frisco? No, my God, the Jackson Square crowd would throw up all over it.'

My reference to the exclusive Jackson Square area, haven of high-quality and very expensive antique shops, San Francisco's equivalent of Bond Street, had clearly excited him.

Belgy hastened to introduce, flattered at this international, no, transatlantic aura on his premises.

'Mr Simpson, Mr Tim Simpson, this is Tony Applemore, good customer of mine from San Francisco.'

'Hi. Pleased to meet with you.' He shook hands across the plywood.

'How d'you do?' My greeting sounded somehow pompous but I hate people who say pleased to meet you and I can't do it, not even for a foreigner. At closer quarters I liked him better, even though the fair hair was too carefully groomed and the brown sunburn too cultivated to be natural. But he was wiry rather than thin, and his face was clean-shaven. His eyes looked straight at you, without shifting, giving that clear, open look that most British people avoid. He gave the impression, that way, of genuinely liking me and that meeting like this was a pleasure. It's an American ability and not one that many Europeans can muster.

If he improved at a closer glance, she was better still. The blue eyes were wide apart and kindly, appraising me so that, when he turned to her, she and I were already looking at one another.

'Mr Simpson—er—may I call you Tim? I'd like you to meet my partner, Marianne Gray.'

Partner, he said. What kind of partner, I wondered, in what sense, and how close?

'Of course,' I said, in answer to his question. 'It's a pleasure. Miss Gray, how d'you do?'

She put a soft dry warm hand in mine. 'Oh, please, Marianne,' she said. 'Are you in this business, Tim?'

Belgy hastened to intervene, face shining, glottal of voice.

'This is Tim Simpson, the Tim Simpson, of the famous

Jeremy White Art Fund. From London, Park Lane, big time, eh?'

Her face lit up and she made mock deference to me. Tony Applemore did the same.

'No, really! Gee, how terrific! Aren't you the ones that bought that collection, let me see, the silver from Casley Hall? It was in all the trade journals.'

I nodded modestly. 'We did buy the Casley Hall collection, yes, that's right.'

'Wow! We really are honoured. Hey, Belgy, you never told me you did business with Jeremy White's, you old devil. My God, that's a long way from my kind of junk.'

Belgy raised his eyebrows in self-deprecation. Our eyes met in mutual agreement not to blow the gaffe that I had never bought from him for the Fund.

'I'm amazed,' Tony Applemore was talking on 'that you would search—well, sorry Belgy, with all due respect—this kind of goods for your Art Fund?'

I smiled at him. 'I like to keep my hand in. Find out what's happening in the general antique trade. You'd be surprised. Things quite often turn up that interest us. We're not only investing in Bond Street ormolu, you know.'

He nodded enthusiastically. 'That's right! That's absolutely right! I bet old Belgy here pulls in some really great pieces from time to time.'

I nodded, but I wasn't looking at him. I was noticing how her blouse opened discreetly towards its swelling centrepieces and how she seemed to be waiting for him to finish so that we could, at my invitation, speak to each other again. I managed to address them both without, I hoped making it too obvious that I was really directing my attention to her.

'Yes, that's true. The auction rooms still haven't got a complete monopoly of everything that's valuable. There are still a lot of pieces that are only handled by the trade, so I suppose we like to think that our relationship with general dealers is a good one and that we can still collaborate to mutual advantage.'

Waffle, of course. I suddenly realized that the magnetism of her eyes and figure were making me rabbit on, like an idiot or an old-fashioned politician, and rallied myself. I needed to talk to Belgy privately. Passing, attractive Americans were an indulgence I could put to one side when I thought of Peter, dead, slumped grotesquely in his familiar and favourite Waterhouse chair. I turned back, dismissively, to Belgy.

'Listen, Belgy, could I have a word with you? I'm sorry to interrupt, Tony and Marianne, but I must talk to Belgy about a couple of mutually interesting matters rather urgently. Do you mind?'

'Of course not.' He was tolerant, pleasant, friendly. 'I'm sure you must. It's been a real pleasure, eh, Marianne?'

'It really has.' She was right in front of me. About a head shorter but wide-hipped, fair, and fragrant. If I had reached out, I could have put my arm round her waist and drawn her to me, incurring, like some dirty old man in a squalid court case, the charge of sudden inexplicable physical interference. I got, for the first time, an understanding of how that kind of control can be lost. Taking yet another grip on myself, I shook hands with her for the second time and did the same to Tony Applemore.

'Perhaps we'll meet again,' I managed to get out to him. 'I really mustn't take up any more of your time.'

'Oh, for Heaven's sake.' He took my other arm in his hand while shaking my right hand. 'It's been great to meet you. Here's my card. You obviously visit San Francisco, so please look us up. There must be things we have that would interest you, eh, Marianne?'

Her eyes held me.

'I'm sure there are. Do you have a card? Just for the

record? It's been really interesting to meet you, and you never can tell.'

'Of course.' I got out my wallet and handed one over to her. 'I do hope we'll meet again. Excuse me.'

Almost with a physical effort I drew Belgy over, away towards the front door. As we moved through the aisles of furniture, at the last moment, I saw some flat cardboard boxes, wide empty packs, that had Korean labels on them, with the usual shipping marks and hieroglyphics.

'Good grief, Belgy,' I said, anxious to change the subject, 'I didn't know that you were doing all this repro Korean stuff?'

He shrugged apologetically. 'What can I do? It's so cheap. You try to sell Vicky repro Chippendales at fifty, maybe even a hundred quid each if it's a set, so the Yanks buy one only and have it copied in Korea for a tenner. I have to do it, otherwise I'm finished. The right stuff is too expensive.'

I nodded in comprehension. We were in the doorway by now and I had him to myself.

'Listen, Belgy, was Peter Blackwell here yesterday?'

His face closed. Trade ethics dictate that you do not blab about other dealers' movements, purchases or private lives. He shifted his feet.

'You haven't heard the news?'

The face was thick-skinned, immobile. He stared straight at me. 'News? What news?'

'About Peter.'

He shook his head.

'He's dead. Murdered. Last night, in his shop.'

The thick face registered horror.

'What? What do you mean? Peter? Why? For God's sake, who did such a thing?'

At the far end of the shop the two American figures were immobile, almost like a tableau set by some formal artist.

'They don't know,' I said. 'I found him after he called me

on the phone, but I don't know what he wanted. He was driving round most of the day and I wondered if you saw him.'

Belgy shook his head. 'No. He was not here, for sure. I was here all day. But how terrible, Peter I have known many years, he was like a—a nephew to me, he bought good things from me and paid a good price. Why was he killed? Why?'

'The police think he disturbed a thief in his shop. There was cash and silver missing.'

Belgy went into the bitter, injured routine of the threatened modern property-owner, calling down retribution on the society that no longer protects its respectable citizens properly and cursing the police for not caring about such things and for not torturing murderers to death. I listened to him with half an ear. Near the door, where we were standing, was an 'antique' Korean chest, a sort of vargueño, lacquered and figured, Chinese-style, like a box of drawers on a straight-stilted, Oriental stand.

He finished his tirade and I nodded in sympathy.

'Belgy—sorry to change the subject—that's not antique, is it? I mean, it's not a real one, is it?'

He was a bit shocked. The jump from Peter's death to trade curiosity was too quick for him. The answer came back like a reflex action.

'No, of course not. I import, what you think? Made in Korea.'

'And lacquered there? I mean, technically, Japanned there?'

He hesitated, just that fraction too long.

'Er, yes, why, yes, of course. I buy ready-made. Why? Why you ask?'

The stare he gave me was perplexed. At the end of the shop the two figures, male and female, stood as though graven from stone. I looked at the flat, cardboard packages, the

Korean cabinet-vargueño, the tiers of rubbishing furniture and nodded slowly.

'One last question: you haven't had any black lacquer furniture in recently, have you?'

He shook his head. 'Black? No, not black. Those dirty Victorian pieces, I try not to buy. You know how it is, Tim. The trade don't like black.'

'Too right, Belgy. Black is hard to move. Sorry, I was just curious. No particular reason for asking. I'm sorry to be the one to break the bad news; I'll be in touch. Better leave you to get on with the business, eh?'

He nodded, relieved.

'Goodbye, Tim. Visit us more often.'

'Sure, Belgy. I will.'

I gave a quick stare round again before I left, rechecking. Experience has enabled me to take in the contents of an antique shop very quickly and, during my conversations inside Belgy's, I made sure that I had seen everything in the place. There was no Godwin sideboard or anything like it. I closed the door with a pang of disappointment and stood outside the shop for a moment, indecisive, smelling the sea air, mingled with the odour of frying chips from a nearby café, before getting into the car. It wasn't until I was on the road, bound west from Hastings towards St Leonards and beyond, that I glanced into the rear-view mirror and saw the three of them standing on the pavement, staring after me.

CHAPTER 7

A friend of mine in the antique trade, out in a country district, once went into his local nick to report on some minor police matter and, as he passed their lecture hall, met his contact, who was on his way in to a talk. Some bigwig from

London was going to give the local rozzers a lecture on problems in art frauds. The London man was actually from the Fraud Squad and the title of the lecture was chalked up on the board, causing my country antique dealer friend much merriment.

The lecture was entitled 'The Antique Dealers of Brighton'.

I never drive into Brighton without chuckling about that talk. The Brighton Boys got their reputation way back and built on it by a system of rapacious knocking—calling from door to door—that persuaded many an old pensioner to part with a valuable possession in exchange for a few notes flashed in front of the eyes. The knocking is not so profitable now that the auctioneers' publicity has made everyone think that they have a fortune in the attic, but the rest of the business is still booming. Containerloads of dodgy goods still issue forth from the bottomless well of Brighton's so-called antique trade, most of it about as antique as my ancient aunt Florrie, born in 1930. Every now and then they do have some good stuff and, to be fair, there are some real antiques in some of the shops, but most of it is flash gear, showy stuff with lots of marquetry and ormolu smothered all over it at high prices for the Continental trade.

Well, what can you expect? I mean, Brighton is like an extension of South London, really, with pebbles and two piers. They called it a nest of thieves when Prinny built his pavilion there and no one in the antiques business in the rest of the country thinks it's any different now. There's a lot of money swimming around in Brighton and you can see that when you get there. It has led to the most aggressive antique dealers in the country, personally as well as profession-ally. Bad-tempered lot they are, unlike the swarms of poofters in the clubs, who make Brighton the San Francisco of England.

I drove across to Brighton from Hastings almost by in-

stinct. Perhaps I felt that Peter's ghost was turning the
wheel, for it seemed a logical route to follow for a dealer on a
run. He could, of course, have diverted to Pevensey and
Eastbourne on the way, because Eastbourne, that so-called
Queen of the South, has a lot of retired old buffers whose gear
comes out on the market after each funeral, or used to, until
the London auctioneers moved in. They reckoned, in Eastbourne, that one antique roadshow by an enterprising London auctioneer took a quarter of a million quid's worth of
gear away from the local trade, up to London, where they'd
never be able to touch it. Served some of them right; some
local dealers had been too bloody mean about buying for
many years, like they have been everywhere.

I didn't think Eastbourne was much of a hunting-ground
for Peter, though. Too Conservative, too conventional in
taste. Walnut, mahogany and porcelain, that's more like
Eastbourne's image, not intellectual or architectural Social-
ist Arts-and-Crafts. In any case, I was looking for something
furtive, undiscovered, possibly criminal. It brought Brighton
to mind instantly.

It was starting to be late afternoon of a fine April day,
rather bracing, with a cold, strong breeze. Coming in from
the Lewes road I turned right, before the sea-front, threading
my way through the backstreet signposts towards the big
railway viaduct that dominates the back of the town. Rightly
so; it was the railways that made all these seaside resorts
what they are. I parked the Volvo near the station and
strolled round the gridiron of streets where the junk shops,
the decor merchants and the decorative bygones all thrive.
The big boys with their warehouses stacked with shipping
trade goods hold the little fish in fee, sending their runners
round on spec to winkle out the latest fad that the American
interior decorators market has ramped up. No one is too
choosy about where the goods have come from or how;
chances are they'll be in a container en route to New York,

Baltimore, Atlanta or Hamburg within hours. It's a busy town.

Time was getting on and some of them were starting to shut up shop. The fourth street, half way along, outside a big shopfront with a side driveway leading to a warehouse, was where I saw the Luton with a blue square patch repairing its rusty back corner. Through the dirty double shopfront window, grilled with wire mesh, the furniture could be seen almost pressing up against the glass to save space. The high stacks were arranged with narrow passageways between them, like Belgy's, so that one glanced up nervously when squeezing through.

Inside the front door there was a little clear space with an oak pedestal desk and some upholstered long footstools on the floor, covered in a Victorian needlework of some kind. Behind the desk was a fleshy bloke in a dark dusty suit, wearing scuffed suedes on his feet and a stringy tie. Clearly, the guvnor. There was another cove, less fat and more useful-looking in jeans and a filthy pullover beside him.

'All right to look round?' I inquired casually, trade-style, looking at them not quite in the eye to avoid any challenge.

'Wotcher want?' the suited man grunted with typical Brighton trade charm.

'To look round.'

'Nah, I know that. Wotcher looking for? Eh?' His eyes flicked over some papers on his desk, not bothering with me, but still intent.

'Furniture and paintings,' I said as pleasantly as I could, while being as noncommittal as possible.

'Don't do paintings. No effing fine art here.'

The dirty pullover grinned knowingly at his chief's response.

'Well, furniture then. Mind if I look?'

'What for?'

I was beginning to get irritated. Prickles started down my

back. I'd had a long day, poor driving, no joy at Belgy's.

'Furniture, as I said. Eighteenth- and nineteenth-century furniture.'

He stared at me flatly, hard, looking me over now, it seemed, with much too much interest compared with his first offhand manner.

'Don't do private trade. Didn't yer see the notice on the door? Trade and export only. Strictly trade.'

'I am trade.'

He sneered. 'Where's yer shop? Eh?'

'London.'

I took a couple of steps forward, towards the steep aisles of wardrobes and chests tottering on top of each other, but he barred my way.

'Wot you after? Eh? You tell me and I'll tell you if I've got it. What kind of trade are you, anyway? Got a card?'

I tried to compromise, to see if reason might prevail.

'Lacquer furniture. Have you got any lacquer furniture?'

His eyes flashed white, then his face settled into a more cunning, interested look.

'What, Chinese you mean? Chinese lacquer? What colour?'

What I really meant was Japanned furniture. I had forgotten that Brighton has been a centre for the 'restoration' of Chinese lacquer furniture and Chinoiserie generally for many years, stemming from the association with the Royal Pavilion. 'Restoration' in this case means the production, from scratch, of green, yellow, blue, red, or black Chinoiserie pieces from almost any, less interesting, inexpensive beginnings. The Brighton Boys will build you almost any piece in any colour you want and try to sell it as antique, including modern reproductions. I should have known.

'Black,' I said. 'Black lacquer. But not Chinese. I want—'

'Nah. Nuffin. Got no black. Don't sell, do it, black? What trade are you in?'

Suddenly I felt hot. The prickles down my back turned to a sort of feverish buzzing under my collar.

'You haven't heard what I want yet. I said—'

His face went rigid. 'Look, mush, I've told yer. I've nothing black. So that's it. Now if you don't mind, Mr London Trade, I'm busy, see?'

He made it as offensive as he could, but my eye had flicked along the narrow aisle and caught sight of a dreadful black lacquer hallstand, all pegs and shelves and mirrors.

'What about that?'

He didn't even look round.

'Sold. Sold, that is. Can't help yer.'

'There might be something else.'

That was when he made his mistake. Anger got the better of him.

'Look, I've bloody *told* yer there's nothing here for the likes of you. Now stop wasting my bloody time and push off!'

Stepping across a Victorian needlework stool, he lunged out and half-punched, half-shoved me towards the door. His left arm ramrodded out on to my chest, rocking me back so that I had to step away backwards, involuntarily. As I swayed, I saw the dirty pullover stepping across towards us as well, bunching his fist as he came.

Silly buggers.

I used to be known for a very good high punt kick, a swift up-and-under when in a mêlée, so as to give the rest of the pack a chance to come up to the opposition. It's not generally the mark of a left prop forward, but it was one of mine; I suppose I wasn't an orthodox rugby player by modern standards anyway, and he was still straddling the needlework footstool, legs apart, watching my face and hands. All I had to do was to consolidate my weight on to my back foot, the left one, as I swayed, and then bring the right leg and foot up sharply, swinging the heavy leather brogue up through a swift arc of about twenty-four inches, using the thigh muscles for maximum acceleration and force, up between the open legs.

Sclunch. Loud scream, bitten off.

There was just time to bring the foot out again as he screamed a second time, clapping his hands to his crutch and clamping his knees together, too late. His mouth, jammed open in a rictus of dreadful pain, made that second shriek and then locked, so that no further sound came out. Slowly he sank on to his knees on the footstool, like an elderly parishioner kneeling to pray on a decorative hassock. Bubbling moans began to come from him.

The filthy pullover nipped out from behind his boss and came straight at me, swinging a right that missed as I handed him off with a bit of nimble footwork.

Handing off, in the game of rugby, means that you extend your left arm partially, place the heel of the hand under the victim's chin, and then straighten the arm, like a piston crank, hard. His head went back and collided with the diamond-paned glass door of a bookcase, splintering bits of it. While his head was still up in the air I right-hooked him under the ribs, bringing the had down again with a cut-off grunt of lost wind. Then, in sheer bloody bad temper, I hit him again with a left, a good one this time, on the side of the jaw. His head snapped back again and hit the bookcase front, smashing more glass and some of the mahogany astragal moulding, thin flimsy lathes of it, that diamonded the panes. He went down like an invertebrate sack of coals.

No, I know, that's not right; a sack of coals never has a vertebra; but you know what I mean.

The boss was still bent over, hands gripping his most delicate area. A high, whining noise was coming out of him, taking over from the bubbling, and he looked a nasty colour. It's much worse when the feeling starts to come back.

I noticed that the broken bookcase sat on a secretaire

chest, which it more or less matched, but not quite. I put the top as 1930s repro and the base as Maples, 1950s. The label had turned over and I could read the caption clearly: Fine Antique Period Sheraton Mahogany Secretaire Bookcase: £1800.

Typical Brighton Trade.

CHAPTER 8

I closed the shop door carefully and crossed the pavement to the Luton, pulling up the roller blind at the back with a practised heave to look inside. It was empty. The wooden slats along the sides were scuffed and scarred, as furniture Lutons always are, and the canvas webbing straps tied to the slats hung slackly where they had been released from the furniture they had secured to the side of the van. Some bits of wadding, cloths, old blankets and corrugated cardboard littered the floor; typical of the materials used to protect furniture tightly wedged together, when the swaying of the Luton can cause damage to glass doors and polished surfaces. I glanced over these conventional packaging aids casually; there was nothing remarkable about them except that, trodden to the van's dirty floor, was one of the flat cardboard packages of the type I had seen at Belgy's, the Korean ones, with their shipping marks, labels, and stencilled black lettering in odd characters. This one had been thoroughly trodden by wet moulded rubber boots, printing their muddy sole patterns, so that all I could make out were some letters that looked like '. .K.D.FUR. .' as part of some longer caption.

For a few seconds I considered going back into the shop and penetrating deeper into it, but then I thought that scuffed-suedes, on his knees in there, would almost certainly have more heavies further in for unloading at the warehouse, and it wouldn't do to look for more trouble. Besides, they'd probably come at me with sash cramps or heavy mallets next time. I closed the Luton's roller blind and walked away, trying to look as nonchalant as possible as I peered into the odd shop-window at the duffed-up mahogany and caustic-whitened pine that passes for furniture round there. I'm not normally that aggressive, you know. I just can't stand bastards like those two Brighton Boys, full of shit and bad manners. If someone gave them a good lesson from time to time, like me, there'd be less bother with them. Besides, they were looking for trouble. I thought a bit about that. They wanted me to leave. They certainly didn't want me to go further into the shop. If I'd simply walked out, as they wanted, there might have been no aggro. It was when I moved forward that the nastiness broke out.

I was so preoccupied with thinking about this as I walked back towards the place that I'd parked the car that I was slow in noticing the two men following me. They weren't just following, either, hanging back, but were closing, so that, as I put my key into the car door lock, I almost felt them, close, right behind me.

An uncle of mine once taught me how to fight backwards, using elbows like flails. Crouching slightly, I pulled the key out of the lock and gripped the bunch it belonged to tightly in my right fist, tensing and half-turning, elbow out ready to jab under the ribs, lineout style.

The one on the left was lean and muscular, my height, fairish hair, with a well-cut suit whose trousers showed the strong ripple on the powerful, bunched right thigh. He was very fit. The right-hand man was heavier, dark, fleshier, his suit straight out of a chain store, jacket bagging at the bottom. He was braced, arms free, glancing quickly at the other man, the fair, fit one.

I did the same, looking over my shoulder to see which way

the fit laddie was going to move so that I could get one into his solar plexus before tackling the fleshier one. Then I blinked, amazed.

Fairish, almost sandy hair fell over the bony forehead. The head was lowered, set down by the hunched shoulders, dropping the blue eyes set in a freckled face which had not yet started to thicken or change, so that the jawbone was still lean, due to the skin drawn tightly over it. The chin was tucked down and his elbows were tucked into his sides, like a boxer's, so as to forestall any jab of mine towards the ribcage; one forearm, the right, was held up, fist clenched, ready to strike. The other, the left, was turned slightly outwards and extended, in a gesture of semi-caution, restraining his partner. The mouth, normally closed into a thin line, and certainly now it should have been, because only a nitwit fights with his jaw slack, was open, at least, half-open, in astonishment. The thick-set man was poised, checking himself to prevent a natural step towards me, although he was clearly the back-up man, slightly out of range and ready to move when I closed with the fit one.

But I wasn't going to close, not ever. Frozen into a backward-looking, hunched position and tense as a coiled spring, I found that I was looking straight into the eye of Nobby Roberts, the pride of the Metropolitan Police Rugby Football Club, but once quite a decent wing threequarter. I gaped at him.

'Nobby?'

His jaw dropped further as his head came up. I half-relaxed, still unbelieving.

'Nobby? I don't believe it!'

'Tim? Tim Simpson?'

'What the hell? Nobby Roberts it is!'

He burst into a roar of laughter. 'Timmy, you mad bastard! You bloody idiot! I might have known!'

He grabbed my hand and started shaking it, pumping

away as he turned to the other man, who stood poised in uncertainty.

'It's all right, George, you can relax. I know this villain. Known him for years. I'm sorry to say that I was at college with him. Worst front-row forward I ever played with.'

'Cheeky bugger,' I growled at him. 'You old fraud. What the hell are you at, Nobby?'

Laughter bubbled out of him. I punched him affectionately on the shoulder and he poked me in the midriff.

'Putting it on a bit, I see, Timbo me boy. Bet you're not fit, are you?'

'Rubbish. Muscle, that is. All very well for you. You can keep fit by thugging up the innocent citizenry with rubber truncheons. Some of us have to work.'

He grinned and started shaking his head in disbelief. The other man relaxed off the balls of his feet, looking mightily relieved but still watching me. Nobby chuckled on.

'What a turn-up. Gee whizz! Tim! Here, sorry, George, meet an old, old friend of mine, Tim Simpson. Tim, this is George Jackson, Brighton CID and a close colleague, so watch it.'

The other man smiled carefully and shook my hand a bit dubiously.

'Nice to meet you, I'm sure. Come to Brighton for a day's Donnybrook, have you?'

'EH?'

'A scrummage of some sort, sir? I mean I suppose any friend of the Inspector's is one of mine and all that, but we thought that gang warfare had broken out.'

Nobby giggled and wiped his eyes. 'The Peckham boys, they said. Or the Catford gang. What a hullabaloo! You've caused real panic, Tim, my boy. Wait till I tell the lads about this. Tim Simpson! Dear God.'

I stood up straight, bewildered.

'What on earth are you babbling about? Are you all right?

And incidentally, not that I'm not pleased to see you, Nobby old son, but do you rozzers normally go about sneaking up behind a man like a pair of footpads on the loose? I bloody near crippled the pair of you.'

The Brighton man, George Jackson, looked at me reprovingly, like an old housemaster who has caught a young delinquent trying to get away with pretended innocence.

'Come now, Mr Simpson, er, Tim. You're not going to deny that you've just massacred two of Brighton's most distinguished—notorious would perhaps be more accurate—antique dealers, are you? Not that we mind that much ourselves, but they might see it differently down at the station.'

Hell, I thought, they've been damned quick. I glanced sharply at Nobby, who was still grinning, but his eyes had now taken on a professional, appraising look. I shuffled my feet.

'Oh. That. Well, yes. They started it, you know, so it was self-defence. Bloody offensive, they were, especially that cove in the suit and scuffed brothel-creepers. He shoved me, hit me actually, so I had to put him in order, him and his mate. Not serious, though, was it? Hardly worth turning out the fire brigade for, I'd have thought.'

Nobby watched me, smiling, but his companion was still intent. I could sense that some sort of accountability was involved, some report back that would have to be squared. He looked away from my gaze to Nobby, who tapped me in the midriff again with a stiff finger.

'Don't do that!'

'You are putting on weight, Tim,' he said, ignoring my irritable response. 'Comes to all you front-row men. My heavens, I'm glad it was you, though. We had a report that gang warfare had broken out—London heavies come down to duff up the local villains; been on the cards for years, particularly with a man like Meeson. One of his lads panicked and rang us up. Territorial problems. They said over the blower that it was a nasty-looking, broken-nosed bugger, London style, smashed Meeson and his minder to pieces, look out for a spot of bother. George and I picked up the report in the car and, from a description, caught you moving dead ahead, fitting it perfectly. We thought we'd have to put the boot in, didn't we, George? Ugly-looking customer, I think you said?'

'Indeed we did.' Jackson ignored my snort of contempt for Nobby's cheeky description of me. 'Quite a relief that it turned out to be a pal of yours, Nobby, I must say.'

Nobby glanced round, then at his watch.

'Better not stand around here. You've some explaining to do, Tim, and it's opening time. I suggest that we go to a suitable pub and we can hear all about it while you buy us a quantity of the very best for all our trouble. Leave your motor here. All right, George? It's your manor.'

The Brighton man smiled at last. 'Best idea you've had all day. Not round here, though. Too near the railway station, er, bit too well-known if you follow me. Let's go downhill to a nice little boozer I know where we can be nice and quiet. I'll call back to the station from the car on the way; tell them the panic's over.'

'Great. Come on, Tim. Get your money ready. You're in temporary detention.'

The last time I'd seen Nobby Roberts must have been at some London rugger get-together, about two years earlier. The last match we'd played in together was well before that, on opposite sides, somewhere like Blackheath, where I stopped him from scoring by bringing him down almost on the line. He was a great three-quarter, fast and strong. If it hadn't been for a surplus of superb three-quarters when I was up he would have got more than just a trial cap; Nobby and I went a long way back together, to when we were at College and played on the same side, thrashing about on dozens of long-forgotten muddy fields and staggering from a multitude of featureless pubs, arm in arm, after many a beer-laden evening. When Nobby didn't get his blue I was heart-broken for him; he was a better rugby player than me by far, but prop forwards were in short supply my first year, so I was lucky.

There were fundamental differences between us which, when you play together in the same side, are not important. They come out later. Nobby was a high-principled bugger, awkward about his convictions, not a pragmatist, like me. When he told me that he was going into the police after leaving university I was aghast, but I understood. There was a purity of intention about Nobby that demanded a practical, tough, social purpose about his life. There was not too much of the compromiser about Nobby Roberts.

He and I ordered pints of bitter but, true to form, the CID man went for the hard stuff. He'd downed a double Scotch and was refilled by a practised landlord before I'd got a fiver out and had to pay for the lot. Nobby smiled knowingly as we sat at a corner table.

I put the first question.

'What are you doing in Brighton, for Heaven's sake? Have the Met given you the day off, or what?'

Even behind the pint of beer he stilled looked as fit as ever and I was sure, now, that he was still playing rugger or, at least, squash. He looked modestly at his fingernails.

'I'm with the Yard just now. Special duties. Actually, Tim, I was thinking of chatting you up sometime, but you know how it is, too busy. I'm looking into some art and antiques robberies and frauds. South London, mainly, but Brighton too. It's getting to be far too big a business and George here is my local contact. I'm down for the day, catching up on local form. Lots of activity here; George and his boys have been very busy.'

I thought of Peter as he looked across at me.

'I gather you're in the same line of country yourself now. One of the lads told me that you'd left consulting and gone to work for some City smoothies as an investment adviser in art and antiques. Quite a surprise.' He made it sound as though I'd deserted the approved rocky road for the primrose way. Nobby always was high-minded, like I say. He'll be a Commissioner of Police or something one day.

'Yes,' I said, without apology, 'I work for Jeremy White. Park Lane, actually, not the City. Always hated the City; we are allied to White's Bank, at a distance. But what a coincidence; it's great to see you.'

He nodded, but gave me an inquiring stare. 'So what are you doing in Brighton? What was the trouble with Meeson all about?'

'I was looking for furniture. Investment stuff. He got bloody offensive for some reason, so I had to clobber him. Your glasses are empty. I'll get us a refill.'

They sat without speaking as I went to the bar and returned with fresh drinks. Nobby then spoke again.

'What about the minder? The one you clouted? He was supposed to be a pro.'

I shrugged. 'When I booted his boss he went for me so I had to deal with him. What else could I do?'

He smiled. 'You haven't changed, have you, Tim? What were you looking for?'

I hesitated. 'Furniture, as I told you. We buy pieces for our Art Fund.'

The last of George Jackson's third double Scotch, on its way to his lips, stopped. His voice held disbelief at bay.

'Odd place, Meeson's, for a London art investment man to come looking. I'd have thought his stuff was all rubbish, isn't it?'

'Yes. As far as I can see. I was just trying to look round.'

'In Brighton? For anything special?'

What were they driving at? Why? I took a swallow of bitter

to gain time while I thought. These two saw the antique trade from a completely different angle from me. Every answer would be matched up against some private measuring rod, some set of facts that I'd never hold. To them, I was part of the whole deceptive scene, an upper aquatic stimulus that gave sharks like Meeson and his ilk a distanced living as part of the same huge murky ocean. There was no reason why an investment adviser shouldn't poke around Brighton, but, to them, it didn't make sense. An investment adviser would be too expensive, too close to the London scene, to waste his valuable time in Brighton junkshops. He would pay runners, give the Peter Blackwells a living, rather than do that.

They were waiting.

'I was looking,' I said, a bit wearily, 'for a Godwin sideboard.'

Their expressions didn't change.

'A what?' asked Nobby. 'What the hell is a Godwin sideboard?'

So I told him. And I told him about Peter Blackwell and the phone call and the Visa receipt on the spike, dated yesterday, and my trip to Hastings. He got quite cross.

'Did you tell the South Ken boys about this?' he demanded incredulously.

'Yes.'

'About the phone call?'

'Yes.'

'And the Hastings garage receipt?'

'Yes, they saw that. Talked on and on for hours, they did.'

'Good job, too. Otherwise it would be tantamount to withholding vital evidence. And you've no business to—'

'Balls. Cut it out, Nobby. Don't be pompous. The South Ken police have every opportunity to check everything themselves. But what would they go to Hastings for, apart to check the time Peter bought the petrol, if the attendant could remember? What would they look for, and where? What do they know? Like you, they've never heard of a Godwin sideboard and they wouldn't recognize one if they saw it crossing a railway line. It was just a hunch. I went to Belgy's on a hunch. He didn't have one. I followed that Luton to Brighton on a hunch and look where it got me. To a pair of typical, offensive bastards. No evidence of any sort.'

'You could have confided your possible line of inquiry to the police. You obviously never told them about this shop on the Hastings seafront. We have proper ways of checking these things. You have no idea.'

He glared at me. I'd forgotten that he could get so touchy. It must have been all that training at Hendon, or wherever it is that they go, and all that serious purpose in his life.

'Now that I've got this information I'll take it up with our South Ken station. Do you have a picture of one of these sideboards?'

I sighed. That was all I needed. Bloody great flatfoots tramping all over London, Hastings and Brighton with a picture of a Godwin sideboard, alerting every bum dealer in the South of England to possible demand. The price would go through the roof.

'I can get you one. But there's no evidence Peter had found one. None. He might have found something else, another piece by Godwin, important but different. Your lot will tramp all over the hoggin, buggering everything up.'

He flushed. 'We will not! We will be very, very discreet. I'm amazed at your mercenary attitude to what might be an important aspect of a murder inquiry. Matters of this sort are handled very carefully for fear of scaring the culprits. I have men, undercover men—' He paused and glanced round the room carefully, lowering his voice. 'Look here, Tim, you're to keep this to yourself. We are operating quite a few undercover boys in this business who can look around and keep their mouths shut. It wouldn't be like a door-to-door search. Trust me. Where's the picture?'

In the back of the Volvo I always carry a few reference books, price guides, that sort of thing, under the back floor where the tool compartment fits. I debated for a moment. Once that picture was out with the police there was a fair chance that everyone would be alerted. Yet I owed it to Peter; I just hadn't thought things through. Nobby was watching me impatiently, with Jackson, eyes narrowed, waiting alertly. There was no choice.

'I've got a book in the car,' I said resignedly, 'with a picture of one in it. You can photocopy that. All right?'

'Good. All right.' He held up a warning finger. 'I'll come back with you to the car and get it. But for Christ's sake, no more amateur sleuthing. We hate amateurs; criminals we can deal with, because most of them are professionals, but amateurs really upset us, don't they, George?'

Jackson nodded. 'Dead right. Don't call us, we'll call you. OK?'

For much of my life, whether as a consultant or with the Art Fund, or in White's other business, I've mistrusted the concept of the Expert. Whether it's because I've so often had to play the role myself and known what bullshit it is, or whether it's because I mistrust experts as closed, fixed professionals, playing the comfortable game of the cartel, the inner ring, the agreed-rules game, I don't know. All I do know is that there are very few real experts anywhere, and those that there are have very original minds, unorthodox, open to assistance. They don't tell you to go away. So I agreed openly, while crossing my fingers.

'I hear what you say,' I said. 'I'll wait for your results.'

And I looked at them, hard.

'Just remember,' I said, 'Peter was a friend of mine. I'll be following your progress with great interest.'

We had another drink and then Nobby walked back to the

car with me, making small talk and catching up on the gossip about old friends. I opened up and gave him the book.

'I never asked,' I said, because I'd assumed it, 'how Gillian and the infant were prospering?'

'Just fine,' he said enthusiastically. Nobby had been married for about five years. 'Fine. We're expecting another.'

I was amused. 'We are, are we? Congratulations. When?'

He blushed. 'In August. I suppose, Tim, you're not—I mean, I was sorry about Carol, but I suppose you're not—'

'No,' I said. 'I'm not.'

CHAPTER 9

In Jeremy's office the eighteenth-century, blue-coated, full-length portrait of his ancestor, founder of White's Bank, looked down elegantly on us from its gilt-framed serenity over the marble mantelpiece. I reflected that it was about as representative of him as a photograph of a coal-miner in his Sunday best might be; a posed, unreal, fragmentary concession to an occasion for conventional portraiture. Jeremy's ancestor had spent about as much time in a blue frock coat and silk knee-breeches and stockings as a man in the exotic timber trade, paddling up the Amazon tributaries in dug-out canoes, could be expected to: bloody little. But there it was and that was the Bank's image now; respectable, fustian, true-blue. The past haunts us in ridiculous versions of itself; I suppose that one day, sometime in the future, they'll look at a portrait of Jeremy, still and imposing in his pin-stripe, and think that he was the conventional son of a conventional banker. They'll look at one of Nobby in his Commander's blue and scrambled egg, a bastion of law and order, never imagining the fleeting wing forward and the pub-crawling undergraduate, nor the grey-suited detective, sitting now in one of Jeremy's armchairs and crisply summarizing his researches over a tray of tea. He and his minions hadn't got very far.

'Nothing,' he said, finishing his report and helping himself to another cup of tea and a ginger snap. 'Absolutely nothing. I must say this is exceptional tea. Darjeeling or Ceylonese? Not Chinese, anyway—can't stand that perfumed foreign stuff.'

Jeremy winced a bit as he did an agitated turn up and down the office. He is one of your tea buffs, is Jeremy, and Chinese is a bit of a thing with him. My sympathies lay with Nobby.

'There you are, Tim, you see? Nothing. Absolutely nothing.' In his relief, Jeremy was getting to sound like a parrot. 'No reason to suppose that Blackwell had found anything of Godwin's or anything like that. Anything at all.'

His gold hair glinted brighter than Nobby's fair locks and he was bigger, more eminent-looking, legs slightly straddled as he stood over me. I refused to be browbeaten.

'Then why did he phone me?'

'Oh, Tim, really! Please drop it, please! Try not to get *involved*, I do beg of you. Leave it to the Inspector here and his colleagues, for heaven's sake. I really couldn't bear it if this business went on into another Willie Morton affair; I really couldn't.'

I raised my eyebrows at him, surprised. 'I thought that the Morton and Brazilian business turned out rather well for us in the end.'

He skipped a bit from one foot to the other. 'Tim! Don't be flippant! These are serious matters, damn it.'

I drank some more tea, a bit sullen of cast. It was two days after my excursion to Hastings and Brighton. Nobby had come in to the Park Lane office to report on the quick checks that had been carried out on both places and in South London to see if a Godwin sideboard or any evidence of

Peter's calls could be located. I wheeled him in to see Jeremy as a matter of form, so that the situation would be clear. It was late afternoon and Jeremy had treated Nobby with elaborate courtesy; the best tea set out, the grave manner, the anything-we-can-do-inspector public relations approach. So far, the newspaper reports on Peter's death had been relatively low key and we were not mentioned, to Jeremy's relief. Despite his love of publicity, he was averse to facing his uncle at the Bank with yet another dealer murdered while in discussion with White's Art Fund over some antique or another. One murder—that of Willie Morton the previous year—might be acceptable, but two would be downright careless, if not actually shady. Jeremy might still be a freebooter in the financial world, but he was as aware as anyone of the need for a respectable exterior face in the investment scene.

Nobby's men had discreetly turned over both Belgy's shop and that of the Brighton dealer, Meeson, along with a good few others, including several on the road back to London. There was nothing to report, but I was surprised how quickly they had acted. In addition, it was clear that Nobby had been talking to his South Kensington cohorts in some detail. He had all the main points about Peter's death quite clearly set out in his mind.

'Looks like a wild goose chase, I'm afraid, Tim,' he now said, putting down his cup and brushing crumbs off his trousered lap. 'The team investigating Blackwell's murder are pretty well convinced that it was a casual break-in merchant who got frightened and let things get out of hand. You see, there's precious little else to go on and an unplanned robbery is always the most difficult to solve.'

I sniffed. His manner was sympathetic and understanding in a semi-official way, like an avuncular figure persuading a reluctant junior member of the family to fall into line for the benefit of everyone else. It irritated me. I became aware that he and Jeremy were regarding me with some concern and detachment, like two outsiders surveying a man who, in their opinion, has become overheated and emotional about some slightly pestering issue. The effect was alienating. There was Nobby, seriously pursuing his successful course as a member of established society, eyes fixed upwards on his career, married, settled, somehow confident and unshakable, maddening. There was Jeremy, patrician, generous, intelligent and friendly, but independent, wealthy, part of another, higher stratum of society. Where the hell did that leave me? A feeling of the easy decline into truculent wage-earning resentment came over me and I almost had to shake myself physically to throw it off; it was unnecessary, stupid, defensive. I was quite capable of earning a professional living any way I chose; indeed, my career was of my own choosing; but my dependence was somehow emphasized by their attitude. I realized that this feeling of isolation was an effect of Sue's departure and Peter's death, coming so close together. Events had produced a feeling of insecurity in me that should be watched.

I shrugged, to put as uncommitted a face to them as I possibly could. 'OK,' I said, conceding, 'if there's nothing there to support my suspicions, then there's nothing more to do and we shouldn't waste valuable police time. Episode over.'

Their expressions didn't change but they glanced at each other in relief.

Jeremy nodded, relaxing. 'I'm sure it was all pure coincidence,' he said soothingly, 'Peter Blackwell probably rang you about something quite unconnected. The tragic break-in was one of those dreadful coincidences, those utterly awful bits of timing that happen now and then. As I say, Inspector, if there's anything further we can do—?'

Nobby shook his head. He knew his timing, too.

'Thank you, no, I don't think we'll need to bother you

again,' he said. 'Much appreciate the help and the excellent tea. If anything does come up, we'll contact you, of course. Tim—' he turned to me—'sorry and all that. I think that the—er—Brighton episode will not be followed up, if you get my meaning? We found one or two items that were a bit embarrassing to our friends.'

I nodded. I had no doubt that Meeson and his emporium might not bear too close a scrutiny by the police. It is difficult enough for an honest antique dealer to stay clear of stolen goods, let alone an unscrupulous one. That kind of horse-trading and bartering is full of opportunities for a little fencing activity, both in innocence and in guilt. Doubtless Nobby and George Jackson would put Meeson off my trail with some half-plausible but warning story; you leave him to us, Meeson, we have him in our sights over something else, another little matter to clear up, and so on. I realized that I was somewhat in Nobby's debt now, as I shook hands with him.

'Thanks, Nobby. Much obliged. We must have a beer together one evening, soon. I'll be glad to hear how you're getting on at the South Kensington end. Why don't you give me a buzz when you're free? I know how it is with you coppers, always unpredictable or at football matches, so I'll try to fall in, anytime.'

'That'd be great.' He was still looking relieved. 'I promise to do that. And no more amateur detective work, eh? No, don't bother, I'll find my way out, no problem.'

He shook hands with Jeremy and strode out, still springy and muscular, leaving us standing gazing after him and conscious of a gap in the room.

Jeremy closed the door and sat down at his big partners' desk.

'What a nice man,' he said. 'Old friend of yours? At college with you, very fortunate that. Small world, isn't it?'

'Yes.'

He gave me a sharp glance. 'What are you going to do now?'

'Go home and forget it, I suppose, like he said.'

'No, no, I meant about the Godwin sideboard. Should we call that project off, now, do you think?'

'Why?'

'Well, no reason, I suppose. You're quite right. It was a decision in principle. This unfortunate business has put me off a little, that's all.'

I rubbed in the point. 'After all, Jeremy, you agreed with Nobby; Peter Blackwell's death is a dreadful tragedy, but quite unconnected.'

Like hell, I thought, like hell, but I went on.

'Peter isn't—wasn't—the only source of Godwin furniture in the world. There's the auction rooms and other specialists and so on. I hadn't only envisaged Peter as our source; in many ways he was part of the competition to get one, or might have been. It was just that he was so well in to that kind of thing that one naturally went to him as a major part of that scene, you know?'

'Of course. Of course. I'm sure you're right. One might come up in the rooms. Or elsewhere.'

He fiddled with a paperknife. There were signs of a mental struggle going on inside the blond head. They came out in the form of a scowl on his normally lofty brow.

'I mean—look here, Tim—should we think seriously of other furniture of that period too? I know you made your suggestion with all due consideration, but you took me by storm a bit. The Fund might well invest in other pieces of that era, mightn't it? It was an important time in this country's history. There must be other people we ought to consider—it could be years before a suitable Godwin piece turns up.'

'True. You mean something by Talbert or Eastlake or Morris?'

Jeremy shuddered. 'Not Morris. Who are the other two?'

I ticked them off on my fingers. 'Talbert, Bruce. No, not an Australian. Wrote and published a book called *Gothic Forms Applied to Furniture* in eighteen-sixty-seven. Odd, that—same year as the first Godwin sideboard. Then there was Eastlake, Charles. Published a book called *Hints on Household Taste* in eighteen-sixty-eight.'

Jeremy winced. 'Hints on Household Taste? For God's sake. I suppose it came out in serial form in a women's weekly magazine?'

'Well, not really, Jeremy. It was very influential, especially in America. They went for Eastlake furniture in a big way, but, of course, being Americans, they started calling all sorts of things Eastlake furniture that had nothing to do with Eastlake. You know what Americans are like about terminology, they call a—'

'Was this all Gothic Reformed style?'

'Yes.'

'Were there any of these in the Victoria and Albert, that day?'

'Oh yes, of course. The "Pet" sideboard and other pieces.'

'They must have been those depressing oak things with diagonal planking and bas-relief carving, with improving mottoes all over them, good for your morals?'

'Yes.'

'Well we're not having any of those, for a start.'

'Right, sir.'

'What else is there?' He ignored my mock-sycophancy.

'Actually, if you're being a discriminating collector and investor you should probably go to the source, which is Pugin, sorry, who is Pugin.'

He scowled again. 'Pugin? Wasn't he that religious maniac Catholic fellow who designed the Houses of Parliament?'

'Yes, Jeremy, with Sir Charles Barry, but—'

'I remember. Thick oak furniture with pegs in. Reminds me of my prep school headmaster's study where the reverend gentleman used to cane us, savagely. And the school chapel. Very plain Gothic mid-Victorian, churchy, shades of incense.'

'Fragrances of incense, you mean, Jeremy, the word shades applies only to visual—'

'Tim!'

'Sorry. But you malign Pugin. He was an original and they all copied him, a lot of them unsuccessfully. His structural stuff is terrific. To coin a rock music analogy, Pugin was the Elvis Presley of nineteenth-century Gothic.'

He chuckled. 'Really? I thought they all got it from Ruskin. *Stones of Venice* and all that, the chapter in it on the "Nature of Gothic"?'

Jeremy is a constant source of surprise to me. Sometimes I wonder whether he isn't just testing me with his questions and sometimes I find that he has gaps of a most odd sort in his knowledge. Probably something to do with what Eton will recognize and what it ignores.

'Do you read Ruskin, Jeremy?'

'No, I certainly don't! Not now, anyway. But when I was at Oxford I got in with a crowd for a while which—no, I'm not going to tell you about that, it was long ago and it's not relevant.'

'What a pity. Well, anyway, you obviously know that Ruskin was responsible for the later Gothic Reformers. *Stones of Venice* came out in eighteen-fifty-three. But Pugin published *Gothic Furniture* in eighteen-thirty-five as a means of getting away from all the sub-classical that they were making then, so he's much earlier. The great thing about Godwin, though, you see, was that he'd been all through that Gothic bit and gone beyond it. He dropped the Gothic design and architecture and set off on his own with Anglo-Japanese and much lighter designs. I know a lot of people will point out that Japanese taste was the "in thing" among intellectuals by then anyway, including his friend Burges, but it was Godwin who started off all the Aesthetic Movement stuff that everyone else copied, mostly very badly.'

'Burges? That's that expensive fancy-dress painted furniture.' Jeremy was quite irritable. 'Don't like it.'

I tried to haul his attention back to my theme. I was warming to it by now.

'Burges is a bit of a design backwater, yes, Jeremy, and painted fancy-dress is not a bad description, and it fetches enormous prices in the rooms now, but it is a bit of an anachronism, I agree.'

His brow was clearing.

'Damn it, you were right, Tim. It's got to be Godwin. There's something about the Aesthetic Movement I can't help liking. Wilde and Whistler mocking everyone pompous and ridiculing that godforsaken Victorian subject-matter painting. What's more, they spent a lot of time cocking a snook at all that appalling, muscular, middle-class Christianity.' He turned to me. 'That is what it's all about, isn't it? That plain oak Reformed Gothic furniture? Muscular, middle-class Christianity? I suppose one shouldn't say that sort of thing nowadays, but I detest it.'

'I suspect that your dislike comes from a touch of iconoclasm, Jeremy, rather than from social or religious attitude.'

His lips curved into a slight smile and he glanced sidelong at the blue-coated portrait over the mantelpiece, looking impassively down. How well Jeremy and Peter would have liked each other, I thought sadly. Why had I never introduced them?

'In any case,' I went on, 'I don't think you can include Pugin in that later lot. There is a strong argument for buying something important of his.'

'There isn't anything left in Peter Blackwell's shop that we should buy, is there?'

The question caught me unawares. I was temporarily shocked, I don't know why. It was a perfectly fair question, but I could see Myra's face and her reaction if I went up there, like a wheeling buzzard, to pick the bones.

'Why, yes,' I stammered, 'there is a—Pugin table—a big structural one—in the window, but it's sold—that is, I don't know who—and who Peter's estate—'

Who Peter's bones would go to.

Jeremy was staring at me, immediately concerned. There was no avoiding his quick perception.

'Look here, Tim, I can see that this business has been a hell of a shaker for you. I'm sorry if the question sounded a bit mercenary. Let's drop that aspect for a while. You look very down in the dumps. Why don't you take a day or two off, if that will help? Go out of town somewhere.'

I avoided his stare. Dear Jeremy, I thought, always kind, wanting to do the right thing and have everyone around him happy, smiling, pleased to be one of Jeremy's boys. Jeremy, handing out gifts of bonuses, holidays, free hooleys here and there, trips to Monte Carlo, whatever, like a small boy passing round the bag of sweets and loving to see his friends' faces light up, saying to himself, My gang, great, look at us. Jeremy, of course, would think of going out of town, to his cottage or to his sailing on the Hamble and the other pursuits he liked. It would not occur to him that I might have no such immediate prospect to rush eagerly away to. I managed to give him a brief smile as I walked to the door.

'Thanks, Jeremy. I might just do that. I'll scouse round the countryside for a bit, to see if I can pick up a bargain for the Fund.'

He laughed relievedly as he waved me out. 'Yes, do that, try to relax. See what you can find. Be careful now, won't you, Tim? Do try not to get—involved—please, dear boy.'

'All right.'

All right like hell. I might take a day or two off but it
wouldn't be for relaxing. Unless I concentrated now, while
the memory of Peter's voice on the telephone that evening
was still reasonably clear, I would lose trace of everything.
Already I was beginning to doubt that I remembered his
tones correctly; how excited had he been? Had he been
excited at all? My memory might start playing tricks with
me. I would have to go and see Myra, look physically at the
Visa card receipt, make sure that we hadn't both mistaken
the date, make sure he really was in Hastings that day
because, if he was, he must have been to Belgy's, and if so,
Belgy must have lied to me. And what about Meeson and his
mate? They were far too jumpy to be innocent; had Belgy
tipped them off by phone while I was on my way to Brighton?

I closed Jeremy's door and went upstairs to my own office,
with its smaller single window overlooking the Park, its desk
with papers strewn all over it and the shelves of auction
catalogues and reference books. Geoffrey Price had left the
latest monthly management report on the desk and I was
turning the top printout over slowly, not really seeing it,
when one of our itinerant Sloane Ranger secretaries, one of
the pool that kept constantly departing due to social commit-
ments that were more important than earning a living, came
bustling in with a rustle of tweed skirt.

'Tim, I'm sorry. I told her that you were busy in a meeting,
but she insisted on waiting.'

I had no idea what she was talking about.

'What? Who?'

'Your visitor.'

'What visitor? I haven't got any appointments this afternoon, have I?'

She nodded, emphatically. 'No, I know. But she insisted.
You know what these Americans are like. Very difficult. She
wouldn't go.'

'Americans?'

'Yes. The card is on the table. In front of you.'

She pushed a visitor's card under my nose. It was quite simple and it said, quite clearly, Marianne Gray, Applemore Antiques, San Francisco. I sat down, holding it, staring at it until I looked up into the harassed face of the waiting Sloane Ranger.

'I'll see her,' I said, quietly. 'Show her up.'

CHAPTER 10

Although I had already met her, standing by the old junk and the new Korean chairs in Belgy's emporium, it is from the moment that she came into my office in Park Lane that I think of us as starting off together. It's often the case, when you look back on your relationships with people, that you remember the first meeting as being of little significance, so cautious are we in our immediate reactions, no matter how favourable they may be. Waiting for her to come up the stairs to me, still half-preoccupied with Nobby's disappointing investigations and Jeremy's arrogant views about later nineteenth-century furniture design, all I could bring to mind was the fair, compelling impression inside the shop, not the final distant sight in the car's rear-view mirror, driven from my mind by the scrummage in Brighton. When she breezed into the room, my preoccupations vanished.

'Hi,' she said, taking my hand in her cool one and waiting for the Sloane Ranger to depart, 'how are you today?'

She was a picture. The blonde hair was faultlessly waved but young in style. The grey woven suit must have been expensive and the skirt wasn't even creased, no matter how long she'd been waiting in our reception area. She had a cream shirt or blouse on under the grey jacket and a gold chain around her neck. An expensive leather handbag hung

on a strap over her shoulder. I bet myself a fiver that she'd
left a new Burberry down in reception.

'Fine,' I said, feeling a little clumsy. 'Please do sit down.
This is a most unexpected pleasure.'

She smiled. 'I doubt that, but you're very tactful. You
probably wished they would kick me out.'

'Never!' I protested. 'Why would I want them to do that?'

Her eyebrows crinkled as she put one above the other in a
quizzical expression. 'Oh, come on. I bet you businessmen
are very stuffy about people who just come calling without an
appointment. They would be in the States, too, you know.'

'I've not found that,' I said, genuinely. 'In my experience,
people in the States, in business I mean, are much more open
to chance visitors, especially foreigners, than we are. They
like to hear what you've got to say, even at short notice.'

She nodded. 'Maybe there's some truth in that. So now I
guess you want to hear what it is that I've got to say?'

'Well, I didn't mean it quite so abruptly, of course, please
take your time, but I am all agog to know to what it is that I
owe the pleasure?'

She put a hand into her pocket, pulled out a tissue,
touched the end of her nose delicately and put it away again,
looking, as she did so, at the ranks of catalogues and reference books that lined the walls. For a moment her gaze
flicked to the window, at the trees outside and the late
afternoon light. I blessed the Government department that
decreed that the clocks should go back early in April, so that
the light evenings come early to London and life is full of the
promise of summer.

'We were absolutely fascinated to meet with you.' When
she spoke, I noticed that her mouth was wide. 'Tony had to
go to Birmingham—' she pronounced it Birming-ham not
Burmingum, as we would—'to see a warehouse there, so
after we had a discussion, I came to see you. I mean, we were
aware of your Fund, White's Art Investment Fund that is,

but after you'd gone and we talked to Belgy Klooster about it, and after what you said, we got really excited to have met you in person, really we did, and we agreed that we shouldn't waste any time. It seemed such an opportunity.'

'Opportunity?'

'Well, you probably get all sorts of people bothering you, I'm sure you do, and this must seem like an awful kind of presumption but, you see, we really do feel that there are some areas of business where hopefully we might be able to collaborate fruitfully with each other in the kind of manner which you indicated when we met you. I really do mean that. You excited us both with what you said.'

It was difficult. I mean, here was this terrific girl, sitting in my office spouting the most abysmally typical American jargon of the most meaningless sort, like areas of business—always unspecific—and collaborate fruitfully and using the word hopefully to mean I hope, or it is to be hoped that, instead of its real meaning, and telling me that she really genuinely meant something, which for an American is a reflex action like saying you're welcome or have a nice day. All of which set my teeth on edge. Yet I couldn't help admitting to myself that some of it was akin to the utter waffle I'd dished out to them in Belgy's shop, while my mind was elsewhere, so in a sense, I deserved it. And she was smashing. Absolutely stunning. There was something about the way her suit came in at the waist and came out again to the hips, emphasized as she sat, that made me ignore all that meaningless drivel. Her eyes, blue and clear, looked at me steadily all the time that she spoke, so that I couldn't avoid them because, when I dropped mine or averted my gaze I felt, for some reason, shifty and weak. I managed, by holding my head slightly to one side, to keep looking at her without taking the full force of her personality.

'I'm not sure,' I said, moving her card to one side carefully, 'quite how you see a—collaboration—taking place.'

She leant forward earnestly, closer to me. 'We don't only deal in junk like Belgy Klooster's,' she said, with feeling, 'like you saw in Hastings. Really. We have handled some very fine pieces of American furniture—and European—for our clients. I was amazed and pleased to find that you know San Francisco, because it means that I'm talking to someone who knows what I'm talking about and understands what I'm saying. There's a lot of money in San Francisco, really a hell of a lot, and a lot of the kind of people who spend very important sums of money on interior decor and art. You must know that.'

'Indeed. Yes, there are,' I said, thinking of Tony Applemore and his jeans suit and a statistic that I saw somewhere that said that nearly thirty per cent of San Francisco men are raving poofters. One good thing about poofters is that they are usually mad keen on art and antiques and interior decor. Helps the market no end, as many a Brighton dealer will testify. But she was going on.

'—Jackson Square, you've seen it, or the area, and how much material there is, with all due respect it leaves Bond Street—'

'Standing,' I interrupted. 'The stock in the shops in, or rather around, the Jackson Square area, 'cos there's no actual square for some silly reason, is colossal compared to the majority of those here. The finance behind them must be massive. Not that everything is always genuine, mark you, and some things are ridiculously expensive, five times their price here. Yet others, perhaps because they don't seem to know what they've got, or the market is different, are quite reasonable, even cheap, so that one or two English dealers have been shipping stuff back.'

Her eyes shone. 'You've got it! Real opportunities for someone who knows! It's not only that. I mean, there must be Americans who'd be glad to invest in your Fund, but I've never seen it promoted in the States and you know how we are about stock markets, it's like the national way of gambling—'

It was true, of course. Jeremy and I had often discussed it. Up to then we had been too busy with the launch of our Fund in London and in satisfying our British clients, but we knew where the real money is, just as all the London art auctioneers do, so that they have spent millions setting up in New York and elsewhere in an effort to cash in on American wealth. Their feeling that the art market of the world would eventually centre somewhere across the Atlantic has been an expensive one; I've often wondered how the London art trade and collectors must feel, seeing their expensive premiums spent madly in an effort to take the centre of the art market away from them, to America. Jeremy and I were quite agreed that, one day, we would have to transfer our Fund idea to the States, either by broadening the acquisitions into American pieces or, more likely, by setting up a separate White's American Art Investment Fund to make sure that we kept ourselves well up in the game. Now here was this girl, forcing the pace.

'—I mean, if you could promote the idea at the American end, I'm sure—I'm absolutely certain—it would be a terrific success, especially with you and your Bank's experience and expertise and backing—'

The problem, of course, was to find someone knowledgeable enough about the American market, without being too specific or too narrow an expert, to know what spread of investment to go in for and where, most judiciously, to buy. I was quite confident about British antiques but when Jeremy suggested that I did the US end too, I was cautious. His other suggestion was that I might visit the States on a regular basis to build up familiarity and for a while I considered commuting each month for a week's visit at a time. Now that Sue had gone, I turned the idea over in my mind with more enthusiasm, but there was nothing like a local expert to prevent

outsiders like us from being taken for a ride. Our own
supervision would always be essential, so my presence in the
States was likely whatever course we adopted.

'I suppose,' I said, putting my thoughts out loud, 'that the
place to start up over there would be New York, almost
certainly.'

'No! Why?' She was aghast. 'What for? Oh, I know what
you mean—because it's a big existing market now and the
whole Jewish bit is there, that's not prejudice, the Jews are
highly cultured and appreciative of art, so you think that's
where you've got to be. But it isn't so. New York may be it
right now, but the future's on the West Coast, anyone will tell
you that; you'd be starting from way back. You'd only be
following the rest, doing a me-too operation.'

She leant further forward still, nearer to me. 'You should
leapfrog New York. Go right over it. Go for the future. The
West Coast is the place to be; look at the Getty Museum,
that's managed by a British guy, isn't it? Come on, don't be
left behind! You've pioneered your Fund—try something
really new!'

She sat back triumphantly, smiling at me. I liked it. It was
refreshing to have a new aspect of the Fund to discuss,
concerned for a change with its development and future,
rather than the almost technical aspect of what long-dead
object to buy next. Collecting for investment has its fasci-
nations, its pursuits, quarry, chase, prizes and surrenders,
but it does not have the vigour of creation nor the enthusiasm
that patronage of living artists and craftsmen can engender.
Its excitements are largely archæological, to be compared
with falling over a pyramid or digging up an undiscovered
vase. She was like someone who reminds us of the whole
purpose of preserving the past's artefacts; so that we can
develop in the future, not fossilize ourselves. The lesson to be
learnt from museums is that of the insight they may give us
on contemporary problems we are trying to unravel; I had a

sudden light-shaft of intelligence on something that I must do, the next day, à propos of my thoughts about Peter's death.

Her eyes met mine quizzically. I realized that her smile had become slightly fixed and that she was waiting patiently for me to make the next move. For the few seconds that had followed her last remark I had gone into a brown study as the thoughts she had stimulated flashed through my mind. I pulled myself together, quickly.

'It's an interesting idea—' how lame I sounded—'and I must tell you that we have been thinking about the States for some time.'

'Oh.' Her voice held a tinge of disappointment. 'I should have realized, of course, but—'

'Nothing is fixed yet by any means, I do assure you. The West Coast idea could well be something we ought to consider. The way in which we tackle the States will need careful planning. It can be very damaging to get off on the wrong foot.'

'That's right. Maybe that's where we could help you. I mean, I realize that this isn't something you can just jump into, but I do believe that Tony and I could help you and we are here right now if you'd like to discuss it with your other directors or whatever. We have thirty thousand square feet of warehouse outside San Francisco, we're not the biggest by any means, but we do know how the system works and we have access to capital if you're looking for partners. I mean, I know that just bursting in on you like this, you have to be very careful, but we are over for a while and it seemed like such an opportunity—'

'And a good idea. Of course it was.' Outside, the twilight was setting in and I could hear the stirring of people preparing to leave the office. It would have been a lame duck indeed who would have said, at that moment, well how interesting, I have enjoyed our little chat, I'll think about it seriously, discuss it with my colleagues, don't call me, I'll call you. In my mind, ever curious, there was Applemore, her trendy partner, with his jeans suit and his good looks, quite clearly very familiar with her, travelling together, her partner in what? Business; only business? Surely not, unless—

No, I couldn't be such a wimp as to just let her go, so I said:

'Look, let me make a suggestion; perhaps we could work the idea out a little more is less formal surroundings. Would you like a drink? The pubs are open, it being London after five-thirty, and I usually find that my mind works a lot better over a beer at this time of the day. How about it?'

A look of surprise and then pleasure spread across her face. 'I'd love a drink. All this exciting talk has made me thirsty.'

She stood up, reminding me that she was quite tall; up to my chin, anyway, and that the suit showed off her figure just as I remembered it in Hastings, disconcerting to a man who's lived alone for a while. She did have a Burberry hanging in reception, a new one, and I awarded myself the mental fiver.

The nearest pub of any interest to take her to was The Shepherd, where she asked for a dry martini. Over that and my pint of bitter we started formally enough, talking about the Fund and its purchases, how we'd found them, why we bought them and which experts we'd used for authenticating various pieces. It was shop talk, technical but stimulating, no harm to impart, and she drew me out easily, pleasantly, warming me to her more and more and seeming, flatteringly, to admire that I said and how I said it. Professionally, I made no allusion to our future plans, only to what we'd already bought, past history, safe enough for almost any conversation. As we talked, the bar gradually filled with the mob from Shepherd's Market—tarts, waiters, con men, tourists, smoothies, bookies, punters, car salesmen—until it started to get jammed, as it sometimes does on an unexpected weekday evening, with a seething, laughing crowd, excited, drinking hard, suddenly speaking to each other, even though strangers, as though a party was in progress. The noise became deafening and shrieks of laughter greeted every minor wit's remarks. After about an hour, when our own talk was overwhelmed, we found ourselves silent, just looking at each other, smiling foolishly as the press of people closed us together ever more tightly. Her eyes held mine, not strongly this time, but with soft promise so that, when I leant forward, put my lips to her ear and asked her whether she would like to go and eat something, I simply felt rather than saw the nod with which she accepted.

I got a taxi and took her to a favourite place of mine in the Fulham Road—no, I'm not going to tell you where or which one—where we got a table in a discreet booth and had another drink before we ate.

'That was fun,' she said. 'I've heard about London pubs but I never got to one like that before.'

'They're not usually quite like that.'

'No, gee, there's this pub that I've been to with Tony, it's nothing like that.'

'Oh, really? Which one is that?'

'I'm not sure, but I think it's called the cold something, we walked to it.'

Hope gripped me. 'Not the Coldharbour?'

Her eyes met mine. 'Yes, that's it. The Coldharbour.'

My face must have been revealing, for she went on: 'I guess you must have been there, hey?'

I nodded. She lowered her eyes to the menu.

'Then I guess I don't have to tell you why Tony likes it.' She shrugged in an offhand way. 'He's from Frisco. In the States that's almost enough to tell anyone for them to assume that a guy is gay. But our business partnership is very good, perhaps because of that. He has good taste and he's very clever, and people like a lot of the things he buys, including a lot of the other gays, of course, and we do a lot of business with them.'

There she went again. I managed to stifle a cry of protest.
There's nothing you can do about it; the destruction of the
word gay, I mean. My writhing in agony at the desecration of
it was greatly tempered by my joy at the whole glorious new
prospect that the evening had taken on. Tony Applemore
was obviously just a business partner and his sexual tastes
lay elsewhere. I hastened to make conversation in as relaxed
a way as the tingling of my nerve-ends would allow.

'That's in the Old Brompton Road. The Coldharbour, I
mean. Are you staying nearby?'

'Sure. In Wetherton Mansions.'

'Oh. Earls Court Square.'

She turned to me, amused. 'Do you know everything,
everywhere? Jackson Square and Earls Court Square and
Hastings and where else?'

No, I thought, quickly, to myself. Not now; no mention of
the vibes of Terrys and Gielguds and other, more recent
memories from there. If you can't cross London without
nostalgia, keep it to yourself, it won't help this conversation.
The fact that Ellen Terry's niece Kate married a fellow called
Gielgud and lived in Earls Court Square with her children,
who included John, the actor, has nothing to do with you and
Marianne Gray. Nor have the other, more recent, post-
graduate memories of flats in the square and surrounding
streets, with girls in search of London life and fun, parties
and nights slept on sofas or, if you were more fortunate, in an
obligingly-occupied bed. Stop clouding your mind with
irrelevancies and concentrate.

'What? You what?'

Her voice was soft but intensely interested. I was melting
rapidly. She was looking at me intently, into my face, as
though seeking some further information or sign that would
tell her something that she wished to know. I started to talk
again, quickly, telling her a bit more about myself, the years
spent travelling as a business consultant, the divorce from

Carol, then Jeremy, antiques and art. I kept Sue Westerman
out of it. She listened well and I felt all my alienation of my
meeting with Nobby and Jeremy evaporating as the meal
progressed, so that, when we finished, I was more than
confident enough to ask her back for a coffee and a drink
before escorting her back to Earls Court. My favourite
restaurant is just a few minutes' walk from my flat—I may be
slow, but I'm not stupid—and she gave me a promising smile
as she agreed. It seemed that the critical part of the evening
had been successfully taken as we strolled along the gritty
pavement past St Stephen's Hospital and I took her hand
before letting her in.

It looked pretty dreadful. I saw her take it in slowly as I
took off her Burberry and hung it up. I mean, it wasn't dirty
or dishevelled or anything, maybe a bit dusty, but the
living-room had a neglected look, as though a rather solitary
badger with peripatetic tastes used it occasionally for a snug.
I saw her gaze saying to herself that no woman lived in this
room or even visited it; no flowers in vases, no simple silly
ornaments, just books and the odd paintings and photographs, two easy chairs and a burst settee, the hi-fi, the
television set and the two open doors, one to the bedroom—
thank Heaven that I'd made the double bed that morning—
one to the kitchenette. The bathroom door was closed. She
didn't recognize any of my paintings because they are British, Slade School mainly, around 1900 to 1930, and it's a
local taste, but she looked at them, interested, as I hung up
the Burberry and went into the kitchenette to make the
coffee. When I came out, with a pot of steaming Brazilian
and a bottle of brandy, she had been using the bathroom. It
had been occurring to me, more forcibly, how completely
and thoroughly Sue had removed all traces of her presence,
as though, instinctively, she had doubted that she would ever
be back, not even after the twelve months she had tried to
pass off as so short a time. But Marianne, smiling a knowing

smile, was sitting in an easy chair, holding a hairpin as I put her coffee down beside her.

'I found this in the john,' she said.

'Oh, really? It's a hairpin.'

'I know it's a hairpin, you dummy. Don't tell me—it's your mother's or your sister's?'

I smiled. 'How tactless. There's a famous film of John Wayne's where he says never explain or apologize mister, it can be taken as a sign of weakness.'

She laughed. 'I'm sorry. I guess that I should have been more tactful but I thought that it might mean—well—look, you're not gay or peculiar or something, are you? Not you too?'

Very direct, these Americans, almost aggressive; but it was so promising a remark, practically amounting to a promise of surrender, that my heart leapt again.

'Do I look as though I might be a poof? Does this look like a poofter's pad?'

She held up her arms in mock surrender. 'OK, OK, don't get mad. I'm sorry, but you are in the art business, aren't you, and a girl never knows these days, you knew all about the Coldharbour, it's difficult, it really is.'

'I told you, I'm divorced.'

'Sure, I know, but Frisco is full of guys who got divorced for precisely that reason, get me? And this place is so—empty.'

I handed her a brandy. 'That's not true. I live here.'

'I know—just. I saw you in an old photograph over there of the football team. A fresh-faced young Tim. What were you? A famous half-back or something?'

I shook my head. 'I was a forward. Left prop, front row, and sometimes reserve hooker.'

Her eyebrows shot up. She started to laugh. 'A what? A hooker? Hey—'

'The word doesn't mean the same thing in English.' I

grinned at her. 'A hooker is the man who hooks the ball back from the centre of the front row. He's very important. I'm not, or rather I wasn't, quite the right build, really, for a prop. Not quite thick-set enough or bullish enough. So I used to double as a hooker, sometimes, but I never much liked it because you get your shins hacked to bits even more than the rest of the front row and I'm a sensitive lad. Besides, it's a greater responsibility and it's much more relaxing to play straightforward front row.'

'Were you very famous?'

I laughed at that. 'Good God no. Just a reasonably competent player. It was a long time ago—I haven't played for years.'

'So what do you do now?'

'I live for Art. Let me put some music on.'

She got up and wandered around again as I fiddled with the hi-fi, looking at the drawing by Nevinson and the flowers in the still-life by Gwynne-Jones. For some reason, I don't know why, I'd put on a tape I'd made a while back that started with a track of Dr John's and, as the rich piano blues chords filled the room with the sound of his phrasing and heavy left-hand rhythm, her eyes widened and she started to sway, clicking her fingers.

'Hey! Who is this?'

'Dr John. It's a number called Memories of Professor Longhair.'

And Longhair, I thought, is the original, like Pugin to the Gothic Reformers; improvements may be made by later disciples, but there is nothing like an original. I really must buy some Professor Longhair some time.

But Marianne laughed, still swaying.

'Longhair? You're a funny guy, Tim Simpson, a short-back-and-sides man like you, going in for memories of long hair and music like this. Is this for reserve hookers? Look at you—' she came up close to me—'look at your hair and even your tie, I bet that's some sort of club tie that only really uptight clubmen wear—what is it? Maroon with yellow stripes?'

I thought of the generations of blues and trial caps to whom that tie meant so much and the sweat, tension and effort it took to get one. Then I put that out of my mind; it was just another tie.

'Yes' I said. 'It is the tie of a club called the Hawks' Club.'

'Hawks?' She was holding the tie and standing right in front of me, not moving now, but almost flat up against me as the music rolled, with her face close to mine. 'Are you a hawk? Really a hawk?'

I leant forward just a fraction and kissed her. Her wide mouth was warm and I felt all the soft goodness of her press gently against me as I put my arm round her waist.

'Yes, I am,' I said, 'but I can coo just like a dove. When my feathers are stroked the right way.'

CHAPTER 11

She was awake before me. I heard her moving quietly round the living-room, through the door. The murmur of traffic along the Fulham Road never really dies completely down but normally I am used to it, even when the louder noises start, round about six in the morning. Usually, I sleep through them.

She was wearing my bathrobe and a pair of striped rugby socks on her feet, pulled up to the knee. She put a cup of tea on the table next to my side of the bed, carried her own to her side, put it down and jumped in, socks and all, pulling the big duvet up to her chin. Then she looked down at me.

'I have a number of questions' she said.

I was feeling drowsy and sated, with the sort of peaceful

languor that comes to those whose appetites are satisfied, however, temporarily. To stay put, however, would have been ungraceful, so I sat up, pulled the duvet up to my chin, like her, and started sipping the tea.

'Fire away' I said.

'First, do you always have the bedroom this cold?'

'It's not cold. It's cool. Besides, it's April and, look, the sun is shining.'

'It's *cold*. Two, do you actually live here?'

'Eh? What on earth do you mean? Of course I live here.'

'But do you have a country place, a cottage, or something?'

'Who do you think I am, Rockefeller? This is it, baby. The Simpson residence. Do you know what flats in London cost these days? If I'm spared, I'll own this in twenty years' time.'

'Jesus.'

'What do you mean—Jesus?'

'I'm asking the questions, OK?'

'OK.'

'The reason I said Jesus was that—don't get mad at me—an art expert from Jeremy White's kind of gave me the idea of some really rich cat with a smooth pad somewhere, so I guessed maybe he's got a little friend tucked away somewhere, in a penthouse or a country residence and this is just, like, where he takes his pickups, you know?'

'No. No pad. No country residence. This is where I live *and* bring my pickups.'

'Bastard!' She jabbed me in the ribs, spilling my tea.

'Ouch! Sorry!'

'Seriously, Tim, I guess you British don't quite go for lifestyle the way we do on the West Coast, but shouldn't you be making one hell of a lot of money?'

'Why? Oh, I get it. You mean, you're so clever, why aren't you a millionaire?'

'Well—gee, I know it sounds kind of picky—but yes. I mean, you must be clever, you're obviously very intelligent and self-assured—'

'Flattery will get you everywhere with me.'

'—no, but really, you could be really big time with what you must know. Couldn't you?'

'Maybe. If I had a lot of money, which I haven't. Which means borrowing it or getting financed by a backer. You know as well as I do that you need enormous amounts of capital to deal big time in the art world and I haven't got any. I won't borrow, for obvious reasons, and I haven't yet liked the idea of a backer. It's too personal and it can go very wrong. It suits me better, right now, to be a professional, a manager, with Jeremy, who pays me very well. Actually you're right; I should live somewhere more salubrious than this. I'm getting to be like an old dog in his favourite kennel.'

She nodded.

'And, I mean, if being an art investment adviser hasn't got you into the millionaire bracket, shouldn't you think maybe of what you did before, like being a business consultant? It seems to me that you must have been pretty good at that, advising big companies and all.'

'"To give advice is a very silly thing to do; to give good advice is absolutely fatal."'

She gaped at me. 'Who said that?'

'Oscar Wilde. The only man to say anything really witty throughout the whole of his period.'

Her lips pursed in disapproval. Very few women admire flippancy.

'Actually, Marianne, I am making much more with White's than I did in my other role.'

She took another sip of tea, shot me a sidelong glance, and went back to the attack.

'That brings me, after the sidetracking, to principal question number three. You told me you were divorced, right?'

'Right. My story has not changed since last night.'

'It better not have. I remember everything.'

'Everything?'

'Everything. Four: what other family do you have?'

'None.'

'None? Yours was an immaculate conception or what?'

'My father died in South America. He was a railway engineer. I was quite young when he died, in my teens actually. He did give me some very good advice about women, I remember, though.'

'He did? What was that?'

'He said that money was what they liked.'

'He was absolutely right. Absolutely. What advice did your mother give you?'

'Well, not too much, really, that was important. Keep clean and do your teeth and make the bed and do as you would be done by and all that. Nothing terribly important.'

'You know something? I think that you're a male chauvinist. A real swine.'

'Absolutely.'

'I knew it. Tell me, your mother is dead too, right?'

'Yes. Ten years ago.'

'And you have no brothers or sisters?'

'No.'

'So who's been looking after you all this time?'

'I have. No, that's not quite true. I had an uncle and aunt in the Midlands and some cousins and things who were very kind. I used to stay with them now and again.'

'Oh, so there was some kind of domestic civilization you were in contact with occasionally?'

'Of course there was. Then there was Carol, my ex.'

'Sure. Did she live here?'

'No. Oh no. When we broke up, the flat we had was sold, along with most of the contents. She got half, well more, as a matter of fact.'

'Why?'

'I gave it to her.'

'You did what? You gave it to her? Why?'

I shrugged. 'In England we still have alimony, support, maintenance, whatever you want to call it. I gave her a lump sum in lieu and, actually, I wanted to wipe the slate clean, start again. She wouldn't have pressed me because she emigrated, so it suited her. She got a job overseas. As a matter of fact I found out quite recently that she went to New Zealand. About as far as you can get.'

Marianne nodded slowly. 'That would explain part of it.'

'Part of what?'

She looked across at me. 'Tim, don't be upset, but this place is sort of spooky. No, not spooky, it's kind of—empty. As though no one really lives here, you know? I can see that there are books and some nice pictures and there's the gear in the kitchen and some records but—'

'But?'

'There's nothing permanent here. And, strange, it's hard to tell what kind of an animal lives here. There's no kind of tracks or spoor or, or—'

'Rhubarb. Of course there are. Just because there aren't any knitted tea cosies or woolly doylies or whatever doesn't mean to say that there's something missing.'

My God, I thought, privately, Sue must have stripped this place clean. No question of leaving anything for when she's supposed to come back. Nothing. She took the lot of her belongings with her. What the hell had I done? Perhaps she just panicked; perhaps she felt that another few months with me would fix her for life, like setting it in glue, much too early, before she'd got herself ready to settle down. Perhaps, to be charitable to myself, I hadn't seen that; women are only ready for the solid dependable citizen in their life at a particular moment, a conjuncture of many signals that flash the message: this is it, put down an anchor, fold the sails. Sue was still scudding along, out on the high sea, no harbourlust in her veins. At least she had promised tearfully to write; a promise so far unfulfilled except for a brief postcard, announcing safe arrival.

I went on, covering as best I could, 'When you've seen a man's books and pictures and records, his clothes and his old school photographs, you've seen all there is to see. Oh, and maybe some sports gear and some toys, grown-up toys of course, but that's it. What else is there? What else can be missing?'

'Well, there are such things as family mementoes and I guess that a woman would have—'

'—curtains and furnishings and flower-boxes and kitchen decorations to provide a setting for herself. Men aren't like that. They don't notice things around them in that way. Not unless they're, er, like—'

'Like the boys from the Coldharbour?'

'Well, something like that.'

'You know what I think? I think that it's true: you are a real, genuine male chauvinist pig.'

'Me?'

'Yes, you. I think you live here with all your books and records and your selfish preoccupations and your job and— oh, OK—once in a while when you need it you have a girl in here for a quick screw—no, OK, a long slow screw—but just for a night or a day or two and then—'

How marvellous, I thought, if life were really like that, if you could just turn them on and off, like a tap, instead of all that dreadful pretence—

'—then you push her through the door, no involvement, no commitment, no responsibility or concern or anything like that, just you, yourself, living your life, the ultimate selfish bachelor—'

'Instead of supporting a quirky female who'll want kids and curtains and kitchen decorations and knitted lavatory seat covers and all that rubbish—'

'God, Tim Simpson, you are a dreadful man, do you know that?'

I grinned cheerfully at her. 'I know. Just think how good it will feel to know that you're absolutely right and that you'll be able to tell me all that again and again during our drive in the country today.'

She sat up straighter. 'Country? Drive in the country?'

'Yes. We are going for a nice drive out of London because it's a nice day.'

'Where to?'

'That's a secret. It's a mystery tour.'

'Oh really? You think that I would like to come with you?'

'Of course you would. And I must say that you look terrifically fetching and sexy in those rugby socks.'

She glanced quickly down at the coverlet.

'You can't see them.'

'Not right now. But I shall be able to. In just a moment.'

CHAPTER 12

White spring sunshine, warming our breeze-protected bodies inside the car, lulled me into thinking what an idiot that bloke Eliot was about April being the cruellest month. Of course, if I had been thinking, I might have remembered that he was in Kent when he wrote it and that he got it from Chaucer, who was more or less permanently on his way to Kent, too. But I started the day cheerful; even the wrangle to get out of London, through Lewisham and Lee Green and all those dreary areas that I'd crossed when heading for Hastings, didn't look quite as dismal as they had been before. Anyway, I thought, once I'm out of Sidcup there's a bit of motorway past Maidstone that I'll be able to nip along.

Some hopes. They have managed to dig up that entire motorway so effectively that a farm cart would find it slow going. It was late lunch-time when we turned off through Leeds and stopped at a pub in Sutton Valence I know that hangs on the top edge of the downs overlooking the Kentish Weald as though you were up in a Ferris wheel.

Marianne gave a cry of pleasure as she got out of the car. She had been pretty quiet as we disentangled ourselves from London, looking out at the passing shops and the suburban drag where the city runs out into Kent like the smudged edge of a badly-painted watercolour. Suddenly she was right up in the air, in a picturesque village street, hanging over an escarpment that drops so suddenly that the plain below is like an aerial photograph. It's the best part of the Weald of Kent; looking at it from above, I mean. Once you are down on the flat it gets disappointing, until you are further south, where the land starts rolling into Sussex.

She was still wearing the linen suit I'd admired in the office and the Burberry was in the back of the car. I don't know what it is that Americans do to their fabrics, but she still looked crisp and fresh. There were some envious sidelong glances from two lads in leather jerkins and muddy boots, parked alongside pint glasses of bitter at the bar. It was an exhilarating, joyful feeling to find myself fussing over a girl once again, bringing her drinks and nodding approval as the landlord stuck steaming plates of steak and kidney in front of us.

She laughed at the food. 'Am I supposed to eat all of that?' she demanded. 'It's enough for a tiger.'

'Thought you might have an appetite.'

She smiled at me slyly, over the plate, with a meaning flick of the eyes. 'Maybe. I'm sure you have.'

'You bet.'

Through the paned glass beside us I could see, out over the plain, the blue smudge where the change into gentle rolling country at the end of the plain begins before it runs, in long extending fingers, into Romney Marsh. There was no feel, up on the ridge, of the presence of the sea, but my thoughts were roaming down that way, thinking of the silted-up estuaries that once led down to Rye.

'Where are we going?' Her question interrupted my thoughts. I jerked them back to my steaming plate of food, reducing rapidly like the bitter in the glass beside my hand.

'To a museum.'

Her fair eyebrows went up. 'What? A museum? What kind of museum, for Heaven's sake? Out here in the country?'

I finished my glass and stood up. 'All will be revealed. Not far, now. Have another drink?'

She shook her head and scowled at me in mock exasperation. The gaze she directed at me was not just questioning but, as I had seen before, assessing, probing, looking for something that obviously had not yet been found. I began to wonder, as I stood at the bar, released from the questing eyes, what it was that she was after. I found it difficult to believe that her association with Tony Applemore had isolated her from the normal run of relationships, but there did seem to be in her a solitary quality that was disturbing. She stood slightly apart from her surroundings, as though looking at them without involvement herself, despite the grilling she'd given me that morning before what became a very satisfactory episode with her in the striped rugby socks and nothing else.

What the hell; I felt happy with her, so why analyse? It was a beautiful day, I was out of town and I wasn't alone; I was in the company of a smashing bit of fluff. Why complicate things? There were serious enough matters to attend to without mulling over Marianne's motives. I went back to the table, carrying my second glass of bitter carefully to avoid spillage.

'What's up?' she asked me as I sat down.

I cleared my face of the expression that must have prompted the question. 'Me?'

'Oh, come on. You looked like you were solving the world's problems.'

'Nothing,' I lied. 'Just thinking of this and that.'

'Do you always look hassled when you think of this and that? What worries you most? This? Or that? Or the other?'

I grinned. 'Minor matters.' It was time to change the subject. 'Tell me, now that we're better—er—acquainted, what do you really think about collaborating with White's? What's really most likely to be the outcome?'

She gave me an old-fashioned look. 'Now that's something. This is a British business technique I don't dig. If you approach with a straightforward business suggestion you get seduced, then when you're softened up they slip you the tough question. Is that it?'

I stumbled to retract. 'Oh no, really, I wasn't being that Machiavellian, I really meant—'

She put a hand on my arm. 'Tim, stop it, it's OK. I wasn't serious. Relax.'

I took her hand in mine, relieved. The question had been ill-timed and artless. If there was one thing I didn't want to get into thinking about, it was to explain Marianne Gray and Tony Applemore to Jeremy and Geoffrey Price. I had a mental vision of their faces, the one quizzical and the other downright sceptical, at the proposed association. I had no desire to end Marianne's interest in it, or involvement with me, but, deep down, in the cold light of day, I doubted if the Art Investment Fund was likely to tie up with Applemore Antiques.

'OK,' I said to Marianne. 'Forget I asked the question. We're having a day off.'

She smiled happily. 'Good. Now where are we going?'

I finished my beer. 'South.' Americans like compass directions. 'Due south from here.'

'But where is that? What place is there?'

'Tenterden, first. Then our destination.'

'OK, OK, keep it dark. I can tell that you won't talk.'

We rolled off the escarpment and deep into Kent. After driving down the wide high street of Tenterden, I turned left, down the picturesque country road that leads to Romney Marsh and the great open skies of the flat sea coast. Before that, still in the last rolling lane of the last rolling hill, I pulled in to the left by a long low timbered house near a high-banked, ditched waterway.

'We get out here,' I told her.

I couldn't help my nerves acting up. My stomach tightened and my blood tingled. There was a chance—how good a chance, I didn't know—that the answer to at least one major question lay here.

Marianne liked it.

'Gee, this is pretty,' she said, putting on her Burberry as the April breeze chilled the sunlight. 'How green it all is! And the fields with those pretty cottages! Just like a little old garden. It's sweet. What is this place called?'

'Small Hythe,' I said. 'It was once a port. For Tenterden. They brought wool here and exported it in sailing barges, across to Belgium and the Low Countries.'

She shot a glance at me. 'How long ago?'

'Two, three, four hundred years. Those fields out there were once a wide estuary to the sea. That stream, waterway, whatever, ran the other way. It was all drained and silted up. The last barges left here more than fifty years ago.'

She nodded. 'And the house?'

'It was the harbourmaster's house. Very old. We're going in.'

'We are? I mean, can we? Oh, there's a notice: The Ellen Terry Museum. National Trust.'

Her face went serious and eyes, narrowing, turned on me.

'Ellen Terry? Wasn't she some kind of actress?'

'Yes. She was very famous; you must have heard of her. She died in nineteen-twenty-eight and this was her house, at least, her country house, where she lived when she was older. I think she died here.'

Marianne shivered and pulled the Burberry closer.

'Why have you brought me here? What are you looking for?'

I looked at the long, ancient house, settled into the well-kept grass around it, with its slight overhang and vast, tiled roof. Beyond it was a black, weatherboarded barn. The garden hedge, at the lower end, might once have been the line of a quay where masted ships would have tied alongside. I've told you I have a nostalgic mind and, for a moment, the spell of the place gripped me.

Marianne repeated her question. 'Why are we here? What are you looking for?'

The blonde hair was slightly ruffled by the wind, but her clean fair skin and the white throat were impeccable. My excitement was mounting and I was nervous, so I kissed her. She looked surprised.

'I'm looking for a sideboard,' I said. 'Come on, let's go in.'

CHAPTER 13

There was nothing there.

Well, that's not quite true; there were plenty of theatrical relics, posters, billboards, photographs, portraits—Sir Henry Irving, for example, she had a long affair with him—children, family. A lot of books. Her bedroom, dressing-table, letters, memoirs, creaking floors that sloped. Stage costumes for various flamboyant roles. I went from room to room, faster and faster, up the wooden staircase, the knot in my stomach congealing, turning into an acid lump.

Nothing.

There wasn't a lot of furniture, anyway. What there was mostly fitted the medieval character of the place. Oak chairs, gateleg tables, chests, Windsor chairs, that sort of thing.

Of Godwin, nothing.

Well, that's not quite true, either. Looking back, I suppose you could say that the pictures and relics of their children, Edith and Gordon Craig, were something of Godwin, but that was all. Of the man who wooed her, took her off, had two children with her, saved her from the Pattles—yes, that was the name Peter was trying to think of—the Pattle sisters, Mrs Prinsep, Julia Cameron and Lady Somers, nothing. Mind you, there wasn't much of her other husbands: G. F. Watts, who paused at the Prinseps for a few days and stayed for thirty years, or the handsome drunk, Charles Kelly, or the final, much younger, James Carew, either. This was a female outfit; Ellen Terry's own museum, none other.

But Godwin: it was he who designed the superb stage sets for her when she made her comeback as Portia in *The Merchant of Venice*, making a perfect setting for her and establishing her at the head of her profession, so that she was never out of work for the next forty years. He put Swinburne, Wilde and Whistler at her feet, introduced her to the cream of the Aesthetes, dug her out of the dreadful, unhappy Prinsep household she had become enmeshed in. What was it that she said of him, affectionately, to their son, after his death? 'He should have made his fortune, but he was careless of money and wasted it and died very poor—But there was none like him, none. A man born long before his time, of extraordinary gifts and of comprehensive genius.'

At Small Hythe, Godwin might never have existed, not at all. Odd, considering that Edith Craig lived there, in another house nearby, keeping watch like a hawkish châtelaine over the whole caboose. She left her father's furniture to the Bristol City Art Gallery, which is appropriate, I suppose, because that's where he came from. And that's how Bristol got their sideboard.

There wasn't another one at Small Hythe. There wasn't any Godwin furniture, of any kind.

So what, Simpson? What did you expect to find? It's a National Trust museum. Not even Peter Blackwell could have winkled a piece of furniture out of there, even if there had been one.

I didn't know what I expected to find. The whole background of Godwin was so elusive, so insubstantial, for a man supposed to be so important to design and to have been so celebrated. I thought maybe that even if Peter hadn't found an actual piece of furniture, he might have made some other discovery that validated or invalidated the known facts; that kind of thing was Peter's speciality. But there was nothing. My lack of knowledge irritated me. I had expected some clue, something that would tell me if Peter had been there, just about twenty miles from Hastings, that day that he'd phoned me so urgently from the call-box. After all, he had mentioned Small Hythe during our last, fated conversation. I scoured the place again. There was nothing.

Marianne was quite pleased and interested. Americans love the theatre. She cooed all over the dresses and the costumes; she found the ephemera of Ellen Terry's American tours that were exciting to her; she liked the simple dressing-table with its woman's implements for making up.

'That was great' she said excitedly, as we left. 'Thanks for that, it was really something to remember. Wasn't she fantastic? Did you find your sideboard? There was one, wasn't there, downstairs?'

'That was a dresser. An oak dresser.'

Americans are dreadful about describing antiques. They call a chest-on-stand a highboy. I mean, I ask you; a highboy.

We stood at the garden gate, on the pavement, in the

afternoon sun. Up the road, above us, was an early brick chapel, very Dutch-looking because of its serrated gable, but with unusual brick Gothic arching to the main window. I thought of the pew in Peter's shop, the one by Butterfield or Street, and some Burne-Jones windows, stained glass of course, that he'd made a bomb on when a church was demolished in the West Country somewhere. Peter was an inveterate poker-about in churches. I took Marianne's arm.

'Let's go and look at that.' I needed a bit of time to think, anyway, to sort out the implications of the vacuum I had found, the utter blank I had drawn. We strolled up the road, Marianne chattering brightly about the Terry memorabilia as we opened the gates and went in.

It is a church, actually, not a chapel. Very charming, with an unusual Dutch-Flemish influence to it. Inside, it was very calm. I sat down on a pew at the back and took it all in while Marianne prowled about. We were just like any tourists, looking at history, appropriately like the poet's two ruin-bibbers, randy for antique. I sat back in peaceful emotion and turned to look at the entrance door and its Gothic arch, emphasized outside by a brick moulding. Marianne was standing in the corner, reading a plaque with a white and drawn face.

'What's the matter?' I asked, going over to her.

It was some quotation, I can't remember it all, that was a favourite of Ellen Terry's, about life after death and peaceful repose. It was in the form of an instruction and it ended by saying, on behalf of the dead instructor, to those still living, 'to where I wait, come gently on.' It was a nice quotation and I rather liked it; the idea of the living being encouraged to move gently through life while moving towards the loved ones who had passed on seemed to me to be a harmless concept, aimed at calming the bereaved. But she shivered, with her face tense. Turning anxiously to me, she demanded, sharply;

'Do you believe that?'

'What?'

'That after we die we'll find them, people we know, waiting for us?' Her eyes searched my face.

'No.'

'No? Just like that? No?' She almost looked relieved. 'You mean you don't believe it?'

'No, I don't. All those thousands of millions of people, or however many there've been on earth for the last two thousand years? Not a hope. "There will scarce be room in Hell, of friars there is such a throng."'

Her face softened. 'You're a strange guy, Tim Simpson, d'you know that? You bring a girl into a church, sit down as though you're completely at home and like it, and then you tell me that you don't believe in immortality, like everything that makes the place anything at all. What are you?'

I grinned. 'Search me. Can't explain that. Churches are just part of things, that's all. But immortality—no, come on, let's go back to the car.'

She hugged me, almost uncontrollably. I had a feeling that I'd touched on something and had calmed it when it needed calming, something best not queried further, best left to emerge, without pain, at a later date. She was light-hearted all the way down the road and demanded, if this was once a port, if she could see the sea. It was as if my remark in the church had relieved her of an enormous load, an anxiety that oppressed her. She was positively skittish.

I drove across to Wittersham and, pulling into a narrow lane, along a track that led to the edge of the old sea cliffs, now landlocked, where we parked, alone, in the falling twilight. Out across the flat reclaimed land of Romney Marsh, a few miles distant, began the sea, out to a straight line where the English Channel stretched into the distance. I tried to think straight. Over to my right, the hilly promontories, moving into Sussex, half-concealed the old port of Rye and, from there, would shield the view to Hastings, now only fifteen miles away.

Hastings.

'Penny for your thoughts,' she interrupted me again. 'You've gone into a brown study, Tim. You do it often, d'you know that?'

I looked across at her with pleasure. Beside me, in the big, generous front seat, she sat, fragrantly cheerful now, and healthy. She had put her Burberry and the jacket of her suit on the back seat and her white blouse, with its long sleeves, looked impeccably neat and clean. She was absolutely smashing. I know; I keep saying it; but she was; she really was.

'I was thinking about Hastings,' I said. 'It's not far off. I ought to call on Belgy Klooster before he shuts up shop. If I move quickly I can be there in time.'

'Oh no!' She pouted angrily. 'Not business! Not now! Please. You promised. We were having the day off, remember? You said so, at the pub. Have you forgotten already?'

I relented, a bit. 'No, I remember. But—'

'But nothing. I bet you don't do that to the other girls you take out in this big car.'

'What? What do you mean? What other girls?'

'Come on, Tim. Why do you need such a big station wagon, hey? You put the back seat down and you have all that space back there to roll your girls in the hay.'

I shook my head. 'Not true.'

'Oh no?'

I looked across at her again. The white blouse was impeccable but the linen skirt had ridden up, quite high, above her knees.

'No,' I said, unhooking our seat-belts, 'not true. The great thing about a Volvo is that there is this little wheel at the side of the front seats that makes them recline backwards. To an almost fully horizontal position.'

CHAPTER 14

I lasted less than a day.

Marianne went to Wetherton Mansions when we got back to London, out of duty to Tony, she said. They had to leave early next morning to go on another buying tour and wouldn't be back for another two days. We probably both felt that a break was wise; our involvement had been sudden and intense.

She had done me a tremendous amount of good. The gloomy mould of my existence since Sue's departure had been broken. I felt capable again, capable of handling relationships and people and of thinking logically. The morning after our trip to Small Hythe, having slept like a top, I picked up the phone. The line was clear and crackle-free, just as though she was round the corner, not at the other end of the world, in Australia.

'Hello? Who's that?'

'Hello, Sue.'

The voice brought her image vividly to mind. The soft brown hair and the fair skin; that slightly priggish, lady-librarian manner that I had relished in breaking down as I possessed her. In some ways, living with Sue Westerman had been what I imagine sleeping with my own sister might have been like, if I'd had one; disgraceful, I thought; how incestuous.

'Tim! What a surprise! But where are you?'

The tone was pleasant, but gently reproving.

'In London.'

'My goodness, how extravagant! But how nice. You swine, why haven't you written to me?'

What is it that one of Kingsley Amis's old mysogynists has

said? 'The automatic assumption of the role of injured party in any argument.' That's woman's position. You wouldn't think that Sue had left me, alone, and gone off on her hooley to Australia, never writing to me except for the card when she arrived.

'Why haven't you written to me, like you promised?' I countered.

'I did,' she protested indignantly.

'Just a card. Not a letter.'

'Oh, Tim, you know how I hate writing. Always have. I'm no good at letters.'

'Nor am I.'

'Meanie. Liar.'

'Thanks. I phone you at five quid a minute, or whatever it costs, and you call me a scrooge.'

'You know what I mean, Tim. Anyway, I'm glad to hear from you, sweetheart, really I am. You old trout.'

Just because I think of her as sisterly, don't think I don't know Sue's conniving nature. There was a note in her voice intended to lead me on, to retain possession, but she'd doubtless got all her options open.

'Good, Sue, it's nice to hear you too; I was worried. I thought you might have gone down to the beach, sunning yourself in the nude with a handsome blond Aussie lifeguard or something.'

'Tim! For Heaven's sake! We're on the phone! You've got a dreadful mind, really you have. You think of nothing else, do you?'

Part of Sue's attraction is her ability to seem shocked. It conceals a robust, natural character that breaks through quite often.

'I bet you're having a ball.'

'Well, as it happens I am going for a picnic tomorrow, on the beach. We're driving to the coast.'

'We?'

'Me and—and some friends. Some nice people I've met at the gallery.'

She made it sound as though she had, at last, been released from the lecherous grasp of an old goat in order to sip lemon tea with a bunch of maiden aunts.

'How nice and, I'm sure, most decorous. I get the picture. As at the gallery.'

'Dear God, Tim, do leave quipping to someone else. I bet you didn't just ring me up to chat about sweet nothings, I know you too well, remember?'

'Sue! How could you? I've missed you; I wanted to talk to you.'

'I don't believe you. Not after all this time. Come on, Tim, spit it out. What do you want? What's happened to you? I bet the flat's got a floosie in it already?'

'Sue! I'm keeping myself for when you get back. You know that.'

'Your grandfather's moustache. Come on, out with it.'

It's a costly business, phoning Australia. I decided to keep it crisp.

'Well, as it happens, there is something you could do for me, wouldn't take a jiffy, just a little piece of information I'm after . . .'

She listened attentively. Sue is a real professional: Oxford and the Courtauld Institute. You could rely on Sue to dig things out for you in a way few men can do, even professional researchers, and she'd done it for me before. She asked few questions, gave me her love, and rang off. The pretext of keeping it all factual helped me to thaw the ice a bit, and I sat looking at the phone for a long time after I put it down. It was going to take quite a bit to get Sue out of my system.

The telephone sat with plastic indifference on the bedside table as I looked at it. 'If only it were like that': had the man who secretly thought that been me? Had he sat on this bed, a day ago, believing such transitory rubbish? Morning sunlight streamed into the flat, barren once again of any female presence, like Peter's used to be after one of his predatory secretaries had left. He would invite me up for a drink and I would look about curiously and say, She's gone, then, and he would say, Have you seen this amazing Gothic bookcase? Who do you think did that, changing the subject and trying to ignore the sudden emptiness. He hated discussing his private affairs with anyone but he always needed those secretaries to do all his filing and checking on research information, keeping his intensely personal business efficient, so that, to them, it was logical to move from the filing, the invoices, catalogues and photographs to him, so clearly in need of personal organization.

Which made me think; I was thinking much better now.

I put my coat on and went out, crossing the Fulham Road to the narrow-seeming entrance of the Hollywood Road and walked north in the bright light, feeling rather than seeing the pavement-pressing buildings widen out into leafier lines of better terraces standing back from the road until I dog-legged into the Little Boltons. The front garden walls and spacious corners there allowed a decent, suburban perspective view of the big, individual-looking houses, until the road narrowed again, past South Bolton Gardens, where the ghost of Willie Orpen perhaps whispered again that Marianne's likeness to Yvonne might come to mind. Orpen's lady was perhaps a bit plumper than Marianne, but that could have been the pose, squatting naked, holding the letter and seen slightly from above, where Orpen, with his sketches, must have stood beside the bed, looking down on her as he worked. The image stayed in my mind as I walked along the Old Brompton Road, busy now with dusty traffic filling its bright, windy, tree-lined progress, so unlike that darkened evening when I had last walked along it.

Myra was not pleased to see me.

She held the door open just a crack and glared through it, hostile, unyielding. I put my foot in the crack.

'I could just go to the V and A,' I said, taking a gamble. 'They've got it all there, too, you know. Clive Wainwright is a friend of mine.'

He's not, but still; it would take her time to check whether the head of the furniture department at the V and A was known to me, as he was to Peter. The door moved, perhaps a millimetre. I went on, encouraged.

'If I could just see Peter's own copy. And his file. It might give me a clue. Something that no one else would pick up, certainly not the police, they've no clue about this period, practically no one has, and they've got nowhere. Have they?'

She swung the door open slowly, revealing her drab pullover and dark skirt, but most of all the tear-swollen face and the unkempt hair as she stared at me sullenly.

'It was something to do with you,' she accused bitterly. 'Wasn't it? Something that happened after you visited that day. I know it was. It must have been. I can feel it.'

I shook my head. 'No it wasn't. Haven't you talked to the police?'

'The police!'

The shop looked listless and uninteresting in the morning light. Dust on the flat surfaces dulled the ebony shines and natural oak graining. The big Tabard Inn revolving book-case stood slightly cock, off the vertical, as though leaning to one side in a tired pose, now that no one cared for it. It would have taken a very conscientious housemaid nearly all morning to dust the ridiculous Aesthetic Movement cabinet piece with its infinite surfaces and Myra had never been much of a duster to begin with. Devoid of Peter's enthusiastic advocacy and attention, the shop looked full of oddities, churchy, imbued with that moralizing cant that accompanied the work of many of those self-satisfied reforming Gothicists and artist-craftsmen of the last quarter of the nineteenth century. Their superior personal style, their too-visible belief in their own better taste, set my teeth on edge. Only the Pugin table, secure in its unimpeachably-held religious inspiration and design, out in the window, gave me any confidence. I even stared at the marquetry-inlaid William Morris settle with dislike. No one but a bloody fool would build such an arse-numbing seat as a bloody settle provides when he could have good sprung upholstery. But there it was; settles are 'purer' to the intellectual, æsthetic mind than vulgar Victorian comfort; more 'country', more genuinely medieval-bucolic and 'honest' in construction and laudably uncomfortable to sit on than a good chair. No wonder settles were for pubs or cottage firesides. No man in a cold, sober condition would sit on a settle unless he expected, very soon, either to get very warm or very drunk. At least, I thought, Peter had the satisfaction of making a good profit on that before he—

'They're taking it away this morning.' Myra had mis-interpreted my hostile stare. 'That's why I had to open up the shop.'

She made it quite clear that she'd done no favours for me.

'The police said that it was all right. The dealer who'd bought it was worried it would be stuck here for ages, naturally. He would be worried about his bloody profit, wouldn't he, when—when—'

Tears began to fall. She sniffled into a damp handkerchief, lank hair falling over her face. I thought of Marianne, with her fair blonde freshness and lovely clear skin, all over, ripe and sensual. I thought of Sue, willowy and efficient, con-fident of herself, her role, her ability to control things. Poor Myra, wet and resentful, losing the battle now, as she would have done even if Peter had not been murdered, as she probably, deep down, knew anyway. There was no conso-lation for Myra, of any sort. Cowardly, I postponed asking about the Pugin table; I put my hand on her shoulder and she flinched, stiffening.

'Look,' I said, 'I knew Peter, probably not as well as you, but well enough, and I found him, remember? I'm still bloody shattered. I want to find out who did it and why. Life will never be the same again without him. Please help me.'

I took the hand off her shoulder—it was bony—and she relaxed, slumping a little. Her voice was muffled.

'His files are in here,' she said, moving towards the office. 'He never let anyone look at them. I'm not sure—'

'I know. I respect that. He'd only show me the occasional extract from them. After all, he made his living from them, but it's different now. Surely Peter would want us to?'

She wasn't entirely convinced, somehow, but she went into the office and pulled open a filing cabinet. I sat at Peter's desk, in the Waterhouse chair, and she swung round, mouth opening, to stare at me. I looked back at her calmly, knowing that no one had sat in that chair since Peter, on that last evening.

She put two files in front of me on the desk and went out, without a word.

In the first file I found a copy of an old Victorian catalogue, entitled *Art Furniture, from designs by E. W. Godwin, with Hints and Suggestions of Domestic Furniture by William Watt, London*. So this was it; the 1877 catalogue of Watt's Art Furniture Warehouse, 21 Grafton Street, Gower Street, London. Slowly I turned the pages. There was a preface, in the form of a letter from Godwin to Watt, which made it apparent that quite a lot of the furniture had been in production for some time and that it had been widely imitated. Well, that was no surprise; Godwin's own first version of the famous sideboard was done in 1867, a good ten years before Watt's catalogue. I leafed on through.

It was odd stuff, really, some of it quite conventional now, some of it decidedly fussy, not at all the simplified design that he is hailed as advocating. I suppose that even famous designers have to bow to current taste a little if they are to make a living. There was a page of 'Old English Jacobean Furniture' showing a mock-bulbous sideboard and a small design for the same chair, across the shop, that clearly showed Japanese influence. They were inconsistent buggers about terminology in those days, a thought which brought Marianne to mind. Yet when I came to his cabinets and his 'buffets' as he called them, I stopped. There it was; the V and A sideboard and the Bristol one. Yet it was different; the top right-hand cabinet had a curtain, of all things, instead of a door to it, half-drawn to show some knick-knacks on shelves. I stopped and racked my memory; I'd never seen that before. The other sideboards and buffet-cabinets in the catalogue were different in arrangement but similar in style in some cases, using similar panelled doors and arrangements of shelves, even the curtained alcoves for knick-knacks and the same funny square-sectioned strutting with rounded corners. Only one design, the Bristol/V and A one, had I ever actually seen in the flesh, as it were. The others were new to me, although they were all called buffets.

The second file was Peter's collection of Godwin information, in the form of catalogues, cuttings and articles. On the top was a photograph of the Victoria and Albert sideboard.

No, it wasn't.

It only had two legs at the front. The V and A one has four. I could visualize them still, with Jeremy standing nearby. This one only had two and it had no leather paper in the door panels. I turned the photograph over and found Sotheby's stamp on the reverse. Peter had pencilled £25,000 on it, together with the date of sale.

I went back to the Watt catalogue. Only two front legs. And a curtained top right-hand cupboard.

So there were several versions, each one just a minor

modification of the other. Forger's paradise. I picked up the second file again.

There were several articles, from different sources, about him. A photocopy of a photograph, showing a wispily-bearded Godwin in a wide hat. Photos of Northampton and Congleton Town Halls, in the Gothic style, both early Godwin designs, well, around 1864, anyway; before the sideboard. A good article by Edward Joy. A bit from one of Peter's favourites, the section on 1830 to 1901 by Charles Handley-Read from the book *World Furniture*. A picture of the White House in Tite Street, Chelsea, designed for Whistler by Godwin and now long gone. A photograph of Dromore Castle in Northern Ireland, roofless, floors open to the weather. An extract from Montgomery Hyde's biography of Oscar Wilde, describing Godwin's designs and superb decorations for Wilde's house—also in Tite Street—when he married. From this I found that Godwin died of an infection of the bladder after submitting to agonizing nineteenth-century surgical probing. A very interesting Bristol City Art Gallery catalogue with a quotation by Godwin from the *Architect* magazine in 1876, saying that the use of deal for ebonizing was a false economy and that he had to have a new lot of dining-room furniture made of mahogany.

Mahogany. Ebonized mahogany. Why did that stop my reading?

I picked up the thread again. Godwin now decided that ebonized furniture, all black, was very depressing. Too right; if there's one thing that the antique furniture trade have hated for years, it's black Victorian furniture, as Belgy so rightly said. Which is why so much of it has been smashed up, or exported in containerloads. Although that strutted, almost fragile sideboard of Godwin's could hardly be classified along with all the other appalling Victorian fussy rubbish that the commercial trade turned out. I read on.

Two weeks later, in another article in the *Architect* magazine, in July 1876, there goes Godwin extolling the virtues of eighteenth-century mahogany furniture, inlaid with satin-wood stringing, thus perhaps laying down the foundations for a taste for Edwardian Sheraton. Stone me, I thought, here you have a leader of the Aesthetic Movement eulogizing the furnishing of dining-rooms with antiques. I wondered what Peter had made of that; there was, it seemed to me, a much stronger element of the fashion-conscious man about Godwin than the dedicated high-principle school would like to admit.

I found that I was wrong in my remarks to Jeremy about the Continent. The French, Germans and Austrians all thought that Godwin's furniture was terrific, just as, later, they did Mackintosh's. Strange, that; both Godwin and Mackintosh died poor, out of fashion, geniuses un-recognized. Max Beerbohm said that Godwin was the greatest Aesthete of them all, which almost guaranteed it; the Germans and the Austrians said that he was the earliest pioneer of modern design, which practically ensured it; the dying in poverty, I mean. In the Bristol City Art Gallery catalogue I found a very specific description of their own sideboard with a detailed comparison of the Sotheby's one. The Bristol one, it turned out, did have the top right-hand cupboard curtained at one time—the marks were there—but the door had since been replaced. It also had brass handles and fittings, stamped 'Abercrombie' instead of the silver plate of the others. The four front legs of the Victoria and Albert version suggest that it is a later, improved version; and so on.

The last few papers in the file gave me a surprise. Peter had collated some random writings about Godwin from the Ellen Terry angle and stuck them in at the end, almost as an afterthought. My judgement of his disinterest in the amorous affairs of his favourite architect-designers appeared to be incorrect after all, but then, in Peter's game, you never knew which odd snippet of information, tucked away carefully, might come in handy. There was, for example, a description of the Godwins' house, that of his first marriage, to Sarah Yonge, daughter of a parson from Henley-on-Thames. It stood on the corner, at No. 21, Portland Square, Bristol in what was, in 1862, a fashionable area. It was a new house and Godwin had built an organ, one of his hobbies, into it. The pale, lofty rooms had Japanese prints on the walls, Persian rugs on the polished floors and early eighteenth-century furniture placed carefully within them—fourteen years before his article in the magazine. The fifteen-year-old Ellen Terry, invited with her mother and elder sister Kate while appearing at the Theatre Royal, was immeasurably impressed. Godwin himself, talented and pampered son of a successful leather-worker, was a confident, willowy young architect, attractive to women and fond of returning their affections. The theatre, and costume, were a great hobby of his and the sisters were invited to give a reading of *A Midsummer Night's Dream*, at which Godwin's friend Burges and his partner, Crisp, were also present. The Terry girls' mother did not approve of Mr Godwin.

Another extracted snippet covered the misery of her brief marriage to G. F. Watts; the wedding dress designed by Holman Hunt, the gloomy January ceremony, unattended by her family except for her father; the disastrous wedding night, no honeymoon, and the subsequent interfering, superior condescension of the Pattle sisters a Little Holland House, responsible more than anyone for her defection to the now-widowed Godwin. I turned the photocopies over. A page of notes followed about Harpenden, when Ellen Terry lived there with Godwin, had the children, and followed the classic pattern of the neglected mistress of the successful man-about-town. Sometimes Godwin would arrive home on the last train—she had to meet him with pony and trap—sometimes he did not. He was careless of bills and finances, she of domestic efficiency and cooking. His success as an architect and his archæological interests took him away for days at a time; so, it was hinted, did other, newer, flames. He finally got round to building their house, Fallows Green, but then became so distracted by medieval and æsthetic considerations that, due to the unpaid bills, the bailiff's men moved in.

In the winter of 1873–4 Ellen Terry went back to the theatre, leaving Godwin with the children in a rented house in Taviton Street, off Gordon Square, in London, while she went to Liverpool. He sent her long, whining letters and, though apparently unable to cope with this single-parent temporary menage, took in a female architectural student called Miss Philip. Oddly enough, it was at this final, disintegrating phase of their relationship that Godwin helped her most. She acted as Portia in the Bancrofts' London staging of *The Merchant of Venice*, for which Godwin designed sets and costumes. The perfection of the blending of his artistic direction and the acting made her the goddess of the Aesthetes, prompting a sonnet from Wilde. Her fame returned fortissimo. Like Godwin, she was an egoist of titanic proportions, a challenge to any man, never a hero-worshipper, who now knew him and his failings too well, particularly after the Harpenden débâcle. He married Miss Philip, who so clearly adored him.

I closed the file. If I had taken my time at Small Hythe, applied to use its library, researched assiduously, I might have enlightened myself further, but I had been looking for something tangible, a piece of furniture, an object, not theatrical history or art reminiscence. My eyes ached to rest on the sight of solid wood, ebonized or not. It was maddening. I looked up as Myra came back into the office from the shop.

'Why isn't there a biography of Godwin?' I demanded. 'For useful background?'

'There is,' she snapped. 'It's called *The Unconscious Stone*, by Dudley Harbron.'

'Where can I get a copy?'

'You can't,' she sneered contemptuously, despising my obvious ignorance. 'It's been out of print for years. Even Peter couldn't get one. There is supposed to be someone writing a new biography but he's been at it for years and there's still no sign of it.'

'So this is it, then? All Peter had? These two files?'

'That's it.'

I sat back and looked across the top of the desk. All it left me with was the bill-spike, with its Visa receipt, and an inkling, now, of why Peter had wanted me to meet him at the shop.

CHAPTER 15

The afternoon turned grey by the time I got to the Hastings seafront and lower clouds moved darkly under the high, lighter ones where the odd patch of blue still showed through.

'If you can see a patch of blue big enough to make a pair of sailor's trousers with, it won't rain for an hour,' I muttered, unconcerned, as I shut the Volvo door. It was a favourite saying of my prep school's Matron, a woman generally wrong about most things. My legs were stiff and I stretched, cracking the odd joint, on the dun pavement beside the car. I have a knee that acts up in damp weather or after long periods of sitting, relict of a bad scrum collapse on me many years ago. It ached now. The sight of the sea was a relief, after London and long driving concentration, giving a distance to ease the eye upon. Over the tumbled grey waters of the Channel, far out, a tanker stood immobile on the horizon.

Nearer at hand, spray broke around the pier, on which occasional figures moved, huddled against the wind.

The outside of Belgy's shop reflected the line of parked cars and the turbulent sky. It had been no use phoning Belgy; his answering machine took over every time, with his cracked foreign accent asking you to leave a message. I hate answering machines almost as much as Belgy hated the telephone. He never answered it, even when he was there, and he never did any business over it. Belgy was no conceptual type; he only bought what he and his boys could see and pick up. As for selling, you bought nothing from Belgy on the phone. It was cash on the nail, there and then, first come, first served. The idea of mail order was lost on Belgy.

Bits of paper and grit had blown up against the shop front. I saw myself reflected in the windows, with the backsides of furniture piled up close to them inside, as I crossed the pavement to the door. It was locked. The whole place had a deserted, neglected look. Peering in through the front door, holding a hand against the glass to break the reflection, I rattled the handle.

Nothing. No movement. The ranks of piled furniture stood dismally, brown and dusty, in silent gloom. The door was morticed and padlocked, bearing no news of when opening time might be, but that was not always unusual. The antique furniture trade keeps its own hours, mindless of potential visits by retail consumers. That was not Belgy's normal style, though, I remembered; either he or one of the boys stayed to check for visitors during daytime hours.

Further up the pavement the door of a newsagent's shop opened and an old josser in a flat cap came out, drawing a stained tweed overcoat round him. He glanced at me.

'Gorn away,' he said, walking a few paces towards me. 'Saw 'em take the pantechnicon yesterday, latish. Shut, ain't it?'

'Yes. Did Belgy go too? In the pantechnicon, I mean.'

He pondered. 'Saw 'em loading up. Boys and Belgy. Think he must have gorn with 'em. Was loading the Luton, too, weren't they?'

'Oh dear. OK, thanks.'

He nodded and wandered on, pleased to have confirmed that someone else's day had been buggered up, too. How bloody stupid. What a waste of time. Where the hell was bloody Belgy?

Rolling down some Continental road, fag in mouth, goods in the back, cheerfully, like a tinker. Angrily I got back into the Volvo, drove about fifty yards down the wrong side of the promenade road and turned right, up the first turning, not as far as Warrior Square. Might as well cut back towards the London road.

There was a road on my right as I accelerated up the hill and I glanced down its narrow opening without thinking, and then stopped. It was a service road, almost an alley, behind the line of seafront houses, narrow but nevertheless a road, used for deliveries and for access to the odd garages set in the back walls of small, unkempt backyards and gardens. It went right along, past the back of Belgy's, and I had caught sight of the square roof of a Luton, sticking up above a parked Escort van.

I left the Volvo in a wide square, just up the hill, where big cracking houses, divided into flats, sagged in the seaside air as they and their mouldings gradually subsided. It took only a minute to walk back to the service road and then I threaded my way along it, round the parked cars and vans, avoiding the dustbins, bursting with rubbish, that guarded each back gate.

Belgy had good access at the back. There was a wide gate set in a high breeze-block wall and ten yards of mud garden between the wall and the back of the shop. The back of the buildings towered above me, three floors of them, most of the upper parts divided into flats. No one looked out at me, though; seagulls screamed in the distance and a silent one sat on a chimneypot, eyeing the rubbish and the Luton, which was Belgy's: I recognized it from my last visit. The cab was empty and the roller blind at the back was shut. It was a pretty rough old Luton, but the tyres were good and Belgy had put an imitation leopard-fur cover on the driving seat for comfort. He was fond of his Luton and usually made the boys take the pantechnicon.

A spot of rain hit my forehead. I couldn't stand out there, in a squalid back alley in Hastings, forever indecisive. I crossed the muddy garden, past a pile of jumbled junk and cardboard boxes, to the back door of the shop. As I passed, I looked, for some reason, to see if there were any of the Korean packages, the flat ones I'd seen in Belgy's and at Brighton. It had been raining and the pile was pretty soggy, so that when I peered at the shapeless mass it was impossible to deduce what had been put into it. The assembled rubbish, discarded packaging material and filthy newspapers yielded no stimulating information. I stared at it for a bit, thinking hard.

More spots of rain disturbed me. I walked over to the back door of the shop. It had a padlock and hasp on it and I could see that the padlock was tight shut. It was as though Belgy had quit the place, indefinitely. Hastings is used to empty shops, failed premises, plenty of For Sale signs. Perhaps this place would join them.

Ridiculous. There was plenty of stock in the shop. This was a booming business. The answerphone was still working.

What the hell.

I stamped irritably out into the alley and stopped at his Luton. If the boys had taken the pantechnicon, Belgy would have taken the Luton. But Belgy wouldn't leave the place totally unattended like this. So why was the Luton still here?

Passing to the back of the vehicle, I looked at the roller shutter. The hasp was broken, as they often are, so you couldn't lock the thing properly. Rain started to fall steadily. I grabbed the handle and gave the shutter a powerful, bad-tempered heave.

The Luton was full. All neatly lashed up and stowed. Chests, several; washstands, three; a wardrobe or two; a limed oak bureau-bookcase; mirrors, oak, beaded edge, nineteen-thirties. Full to the back door, she was. Ready to go.

I stamped back into the yard to the door, splashing a minor puddle in the steadying downpour. The padlock was closed, I hadn't been mistaken, but the hasp, now that I looked closely at it, had been wrenched, so that the retaining screws were pulled cleanly out of the woodwork and then pushed back in again to look secure. All I had to do was to give a gentle tug and the whole door swung open.

Sick with anticipation, I stepped inside.

The back end of the big shop was very gloomy. Light gleamed a slate-grey colour from the front, between the serried aisles of heavy furniture, some narrow, some wider, so that Belgy and his boys could carry the bigger lumps between. Not that Belgy would ever carry any furniture again.

He was on the left-hand side, cradled in a smashed heap of flimsy cakestands that nestled round him like the construction of some gigantic bird that used inch-square uprights as twigs and wooden tilting plates as nest material. One leg was doubled underneath him and his fists were clenched, as though he had been boxing with his short, powerful arms before they came to rest on his tubby stomach forever. The thick, yellow skin on the wide face had relaxed and gone flaccid, so that the once-tight mouth now slackly leered in a spastic grin. There were three bullet holes that I could see in the half-light, and a blackish stain, much more congealed than Peter's had been, spread across his chest. I had never been close to Belgy but it was a tragic, heart-stopping sight, like witnessing the dead body of a nearly-extinct animal of irascible but endearing characteristics. I was about to move closer, to bend over the body, when a shoe creaked behind me.

I whipped round, only to come face to face with mahogany drawers. The main line of furniture, which had been to my right, was now full-frontal to me. It was a blank, impenetrable wall. I stepped carefully to my left.

In a chink between a low washstand and the chest standing on it, I saw the trouser leg of a man standing absolutely still behind the line, waiting. Hair prickled all over me. The bastard was waiting for me step into the line of fire.

The chest on the low washstand was a heavy Victorian job. On top of it was another chest, pine, and on top of that a cast-iron umbrella stand. I put my left hand on the washstand, leaning over to my left, and hooked my right under the bottom apron of the mahogany chest. I counted to three and, bracing hard, I heaved.

Very gratifying, it was, like dominoes. The whole bloody lot went over with a great leverage effect, the cast-iron stand and pine chest having a bit of height behind them. There was a shout and a screech of pain, some sort of soft resistance, then the whole lot crumbled, down on to whatever or whoever had given way beneath them. I leant over the washstand to look, and knew it was a mistake as I did it.

The second man, behind me, was biggish and stocky, but he didn't try anything sophisticated. I caught an impression of his arm, swinging over from high up before the light exploded at the back of my head, giving one spectacular white flash before the dark suddenly swamped everything.

CHAPTER 16

'This is getting to be a habit,' Nobby Roberts said furiously, glaring at me across the filthy desk-top in Belgy Klooster's office.

I glared back at him and held the wet pad they'd given me to the back of my head where the big lump was. Or what felt like a big lump, anyway. It hurt, badly. My head throbbed and using my eyes was painful, so I shut them, very frequently.

'It certainly is,' I snarled. I was hopping mad. 'The bloody country's not bloody safe with homicidal rozzers like you lot roaming round.'

On a chair in the corner, George Jackson of Brighton CID stared fixedly at me with incurious suspicion. Next to him, on another chair, a dishevelled bloke in a torn grey suit was wiping dirty dust marks off his shirt and blinking. His bloodshot eye, where the corner of the pine chest of drawers had hit it, glared at me in undisguised hostility.

'We should book him,' he said.

'Who the bloody hell are you?'

Nobby stood up, very officiously. 'This is Detective-Sergeant Foster of Hastings CID,' he said. 'I can advise you that you damn nearly crushed him.'

'Good.'

'That's it!' yelled Foster, rolling the red eye. 'You're nicked! Assaulting a police officer! Probably murder too. Major suspect at the scene of a very serious crime. Breaking and entering. I'm—'

'Belt up, you stupid burke. Bloody twit. I'll—'

'Stop that! That's enough.' Nobby Roberts's voice was

commanding. 'We'll conduct this properly, in a professional manner.'

He leant over the desk and looked down at me with cold anger. Bloody cheek. I shifted the pad as I answered. 'Oh, will you? About bloody time. When you're not sneaking up on people in the street like a bunch of footpads you're skulking about in the back of furniture stores like a bunch of Chicago bootleggers. What the hell is the matter with you people? Why don't you identify yourselves as policemen, like any decent set of woodentops? Eh?'

His face stiffened. 'We don't usually get assaulted before we have a chance! Anyway, I'm asking the questions. What the blazes are you doing here? I told you—'

'What do you mean, what am I doing here, you arrogant bugger? What the hell are you doing here? Prowling about in your great squeaky police boots? Eh? Why aren't you up in London, where you're supposed to be? Every time I come down to the coast I get attacked by you and your thugs. It's a disgrace. You're all barking mad. Bashing people over the head. What in flaming hell d'you mean by it?'

I jerked my head towards the store, but a stab of agony checked the movement halfway. I could hear sounds of men moving about and guessed that they were dealing with the dead Belgy. I preferred not to think about that. The head was agony.

Nobby's voice was cold. 'I have told you that I am attached to Scotland Yard on special duties and that's all I'm telling you. What I—we—want to know is what you were doing here and why you came into this shop when it was so clearly closed?'

'Breaking and entering,' the Hastings man, Foster, said savagely, mopping at his eye now. 'Let me have him, Chief. He can take the lot. Resisting a police officer in the course of—'

'Oh, drop dead.'

'Now look here, chummy, you're in serious trouble, d'you know that? You better start explaining—'

I started to get up. 'Call me chummy once again, Fartinbrass, or whatever your name is, and I'll break your fucking—'

'Stop it! Sit down!'

Nobby was shouting. Jackson stifled a grin.

'Sergeant Foster is quite correct! A murder has been committed here and you break into the premises like a common criminal! If you can't give a reasonable explanation, then I shall have to agree that you be cautioned and taken to the police station.'

He was very defensive. Poor Nobby; I'd put him in a spot. By turning the wet pad over, I managed to get another cold area to press on to the damage at the back of my head. It didn't feel as though the skin was broken, fortunately, and the lump might subside if I kept cooling it. I scowled at Jackson, who gave me a pleasant smile; he was obviously the one who'd hit me. They were waiting.

'Look,' I said wearily, 'the breaking and entering bit won't stick and you know it. The door was open. Someone broke the lock—you, I imagine—and I came in. So I didn't break in. I've known Belgy Klooster for a long time and it's perfectly reasonable for me to come in, even when he isn't here. Actually, I guessed that he was in here because the Luton outside is loaded up and he'd never leave it like that, unlocked, for long. I thought he was in here, just getting his bits and pieces together before leaving. So I came in. You know the rest. I thought you were the enemy. If you'd said out loud that you were the Force instead of skulking about, all this would never have happened.'

Jackson shifted in his chair, glanced at Nobby and nodded.

A thought occurred to me. 'I suppose that old josser outside was one of yours?'

'Yes.'

'Well then, what the blazes do you mean by it? I might just sue you, d'you know that?'

Foster of Hastings gaped at me incredulously. Nobby closed his eyes for a moment.

'Well? Explain, dammit!'

He opened them again.

'It's all a bit of a coincidence. We wanted to interview Klooster about various—er—matters. We had a report that he'd gone away, but when some friends of yours in the Belgian police stopped his two lads in their big van, they said he was still in Hastings looking after the shop. They said they'd helped him to load the Luton for a local delivery before they left. We came here to find him and saw the padlocked door, which seemed odd to us too. Since we were looking for stolen goods, we had no problem about authority to enter. George here pulled the hasp screws out. We found more than we bargained for. It's interesting that he might have been here, dead, for over a week before the boys were due back. The man we posted outside said there was a prowler—smooth-looking thug was his description—so we took cover to see what it was all about. And in came you. Again.'

He shoved his hands in his pockets, took out a handkerchief, blew the dust out of his nose and looked at me irritably.

'I'm still waiting. Why were you here? Don't tell me or George, this time, that you were looking for antiques. Not here. The truth, please.'

'Just one more question. Why did you want to see Belgy?'

He looked at George Jackson before replying.

'We don't know, yet. I've told you that I'm on special duties, looking into frauds and other crimes connected with the art and antiques trade. Klooster was an oddball, on my list of suspects. He travelled in and out of the country a hell of a lot. There were several things he was probably involved in, possibly drugs, certainly stolen goods. Houses in a wide area around here got cleared out and the stuff just disappeared. Furniture, silver, paintings, clocks, the lot. It all had to be going to the Continent. Klooster was a prime suspect.'

'Christ. Why didn't you just pick him up?'

All three of them smiled thinly. George Jackson spoke up.

'Have you any idea how many men we have available to follow up all that gear and stop vans and compare photographs and all that? To cover the whole of South-East England? The chances of recovering stolen goods are getting so slight that it's becoming a growth industry. Men like Klooster aren't stupid—sorry—weren't stupid. They'd hit a house when people were away and be on the ferry, manifest, invoices and all, within hours. Like three hours. By the time the folks were back off holiday or found out they'd been hit and the local police started making inquiries, dealers like Klooster would have sold the stuff in Holland or wherever and be back sitting down to breakfast in Hastings.'

He leant forward across the table and glared at me.

'The Rye police have two cars to cover God knows how many square miles. In one area here the local village police have a mileage budget for their motor bikes or vehicles, so if they go over they have to walk for a week or so. See a village bobby walking round here and the chances are that he's used up his petrol budget for the month. It leaked to one set of villains and they moved about five containerloads that week while the petrol ban was on.'

The Hastings man spoke up, still watching me hungrily.

'You could pick up men like Klooster till you was blue in the face. You'd waste your time. Only luck or a tip-off'd get you a charge that would stick. All the antique trade are bent, everyone knows that, but it's catching them that's the problem. They have to fall out among themselves, the one'll rat on the other.'

'So did Belgy and someone fall out? Who?'

'Dunno. I reckon we've answered enough of your questions now, anyway. It's time you did a bit of explaining.'

I braced myself. They weren't going to like it, so I started carefully.

'Peter Blackwell,' I said, 'was here the day he died. I just know he was.'

Nobby rolled his eyes up to the ceiling. 'Oh no! I don't believe it! I thought that we had straightened all that out when I left you and Jeremy White at your offices. You agreed then that there was no point in pursuing that line of inquiry. You agreed, damn it!'

'I changed my mind.'

'For God's sake why? Why?'

'He was in this area. The garage receipt confirms it. He didn't go to another, alternative place nearby, Small Hythe, or even if he did, there was nothing there to excite him, so—'

'Wait! Wait! Small Hythe? What or where is Small Hythe?'

'The Ellen Terry Museum, near Tenterden, I thought he might have been there on his rounds, so I went in and checked. There's nothing of Godwin's there. It wasn't that visit—if he made it—that led to his call to me. It was something here, or maybe elsewhere, but whatever it was, Belgy lied to me. He lied to me, saying that Peter hadn't been here when it's a stone cold racing certainty that he had. I'd been to Small Hythe yesterday—'

'Pursuing your independent line of inquiry, I assume—'

'There's no need to be sarcastic. From what you've just said about your resources, you should be thanking me for saving you the bother, and I was going to come on here afterwards.'

'So why didn't you, Sherlock?' Foster was no friendlier.

'I—er—I got diverted.'

'So you decided to carry on the amateur sleuthing and come here today.' Nobby sounded just as unfriendly.

'Something like that, maybe. I just wanted to press Belgy, to find out what the hell it was all about.'

'It couldn't have been, perhaps—' Nobby was getting sarcastic now—'that Klooster had found and sold a Godwin piece that he didn't want to talk about and you and Blackwell wanted to get your hands on it? So that you are still looking for it now? Hoping to get Klooster to tell you where it is? I must say you were damned reluctant to talk about the whole subject in Brighton; it was obviously more important to you than seeing justice pursued unhampered.'

'Oh Gawd, Nobby, do you lecture in Sunday School nowadays as well? I don't understand it all, that's my problem. If Klooster had one, why wouldn't he sell it to Peter? Why hide it?'

'Because it would almost certainly be nicked.' Foster's voice was irritable. 'A lot of Belgy Klooster's stuff was nicked. Not that that would bother your London dealer friend, I'm sure. Or you. All antique dealers are bent; and those who deal with them.' He leered at me meaningly.

'Now see here, PC Plod, you keep your bloody—'

'Stop it!' Nobby's voice was dismissive. 'There's plenty to do outside. You two—' he gestured at Jackson and Foster—'had better go out there and help the rest. I'll join you in a moment. There are a couple of matters I'll finish off with Mr Simpson.'

They left. Foster didn't give me more than a hostile stare but Jackson still had his incurious, humorous, speculative look. He nodded as he went. Nobby shifted uneasily, waiting for them to go, then he looked at me in steady detachment, keeping his face stern.

'This is getting very difficult and embarrassing,' he said.

'You bet it is. If you and your gang keep attacking people this way, one day you'll hit someone who isn't an old friend and get yourselves into trouble.'

'Cut it out, Tim! You know damn well what I mean!

Because I know you so well, my colleagues are starting to think that I'm not dealing with you correctly, with detachment and objectivity. That our friendship may be prejudicing my judgement in this case.'

'For God's sake stop being so pompous Nobby. Everyone can see that—'

'See? Can they? What can they see? That you are involved in some sort of shady business? Two murders, violence among known receivers of stolen goods, is that what they can see or isn't it?'

'That's ridiculous. And you can't have it both ways. You said it was all coincidence in the first place. I'm a perfectly innocent outsider who's stumbled on two unfortunate— and unconnected, according to you—murders. By pure chance.'

'Chance? Have you thought about your position? It's only chance perhaps, we don't know, but a chance caused by the field in which you operate, Tim. With art dealers and antique-mongers and all the bent fringe-dwellers who hang on to that world. Blackwell did the same; the South Ken police said that he mixed with some very rum types while in the line of business and that's what you've become, too. Tell me who you are with and I'll tell you who you are.'

'That's absurd! Crazy! You're off your trolley. You've been in the police too long, that's your trouble. If I were a banker I suppose you'd say that was suspicious too, because bankers handle money and everyone knows that money leads to crime.'

'This is different. I'm getting to know the antique trade, you wouldn't believe the things I know.'

'I bet I would. It doesn't mean to say that I'm involved in them. Don't spout your Puritan morality at me. You know, you always had a tendency that way. I'm bloody disappointed in you, Nobby; you'll end up advertising tyres on TV.'

He flushed. His mouth snapped shut. I put the wet pad down and stood up shakily.

'I take it,' I said sarcastically, 'that I am free to go? I mean, I won't get tackled as I go through the door, or truncheoned at my car, will I?'

His mouth went into a thin line. He's not a bad fellow, Nobby, but you must not let him get all toffee-nosed.

'We'll need a statement from you. Not now. Look, Tim, I just don't like to think of you going down the wrong path, that's all. You do know what you're doing, don't you?'

'Yes.'

'Then please stay out of detective work and leave it to us. Forget it.'

'Why? Have you got the faintest idea who killed Peter?'

He went white with anger. 'My God, but you're an aggressive bastard! Well, I've warned you! Stay out of this or there'll be trouble! That's the last time!'

We walked out into the furniture store, where the photographers and others worked in a mundane fashion, as though dealing with bodies was an everyday occurrence. George Jackson grinned at me as Nobby stalked off angrily to deal with his other minions, turning his back to me, deliberately.

'Had a wigging from sir? You and he seem to be sparring a bit, for old friends.'

I smiled crookedly back. 'Something like that.' We looked across at the covered form of Belgy Klooster. 'Who would have killed him?'

Jackson shook his head. 'He was involved in a lot of things. Usually it doesn't take long to find out. We'll be going through all the well-tried forensic work and the routine checks. I'm sorry about the head, by the way.'

'No umbrage taken. When do they think it happened?'

'Very late, they reckon. Some time around midnight. He must have been working after hours. Whoever killed him just shut up the shop and left. It was good timing; might have been a few days before he was found.'

They were wrapping up the body and taking it away, so that we had to stand to one side. Nobby came up to us as the stretcher passed.

'Anything more?' he asked Jackson, who shook his head.

'Only this. It was clutched in his hand.'

He held out a crumpled brown object, screwed into a wrinkled ball. I looked at it and then made my way to the back alley, pondering. It was nothing important, just a piece of cardboard from a flat cardboard carton, but, as I got to the car and opened the door, it occurred to me how like any other piece of Oriental furniture a Godwin sideboard would look, if it were put together in that raw Korean mahogany.

CHAPTER 17

Two mornings later, after I had brought in some coffee and a slice of toast each, checked that the heating was on, and slid back into bed, the image of Willie Orpen's blonde was vividly back in mind. The painting shows her as you would see her from normal height, if you were standing by the bed, looking down. She sits quite naturally, as I have told you already, back on her haunches, knees apart; no, it's not a shocking painting or anything like that, just very natural; and she is reading the letter, in fact that's the title of the painting—*The Letter*—and Marianne looked just like that.

It had been a bad night. Having to tell Marianne about Belgy hadn't helped. She was very shocked, more than I had expected, and quizzed me in a way that was a bit vicarious, as though her horror demanded every detail. Later, after I listened to her breathing become regular and heavy, relaxed in sleep, I had had fitful dozes, brief snatches, between awful waking starts. Every time I slipped off, the image of Belgy, yellowy-grey face collapsed in death, came leering up at me from the surrounding dark. Every noise in the Fulham Road woke me, cursing and vowing that I would move, soon, away from the seedy locality and the shifting traffic. I could afford to move; why shouldn't I? Perhaps Marianne would come over regularly; perhaps Sue would come back; no, I somehow didn't think Sue would come back, and anyway Marianne was much better in bed than Sue, more inventive, less bloody reserved and English, more, well, more foreign, I suppose. More natural about it. She had a terrific figure. Thinking about that, I slipped into sleep again and there was Belgy back, crumpled up amid the smashed bits of wood, and Peter was looking down at him, puffing on a cigarette and saying something about black being bad for business unless you could put a name to it and then there was a fortune to be made but not for the Aesthetic Movement, they all came to a bad end or were bankrupted, look at Wilde and Whistler and Godwin . . . I was bloody glad when morning came.

Marianne set up quite casually, relaxed and tousled, knees apart and drawn up, the cup of coffee on the bed between them, looking with domestic calm at me and the room about her. The sense of *déjà vu* was very powerful. Her fair skin was unblemished and the shortish, yellow hair curled round the nape of her neck, leaving a long shapely back quite clear of any entanglement. I put my arm around her naked waist.

She seemed slightly amused as she looked across at me. I had propped myself up against the pillows, sheet decorously over my lap, and was half-lying, upright enough to drink my coffee from a mug without spilling.

'You all right?' she queried impishly.

You never know quite what they mean or are getting at, do you?

'Yes of course, great. Why?'

She smiled knowingly. 'You seemed a bit tense, last night. You know when I mean. Just a bit—tense.'

'Me? Never. I—'

The phone rang. Muttering a curse but blessing the interruption, I put my cup on one side, took my arm away from her waist and leant over the bedside table to unhook the receiver. She waited, cup in hand.

There were a few bleeps and then an echoing, then the line cleared. It had to be long distance.

'Tim? Is that you?'

Oh my God. Sue Westerman, from Australia.

'Yes, it's Tim here. How are you?'

I tried to keep my voice normal, matter of fact, and not to use Sue's name. Marianne put her cup down.

'Are you all right? You sound a bit funny.'

'Yes I'm fine, thanks. How are you?'

Marianne poked me playfully in the ribs. Sue's voice bleeped on.

'I've just told you I'm fine. Listen, Tim—'

Marianne, unencumbered of cup, moved across the bed close to me and slid a hand under the sheet. I jumped spasmodically and clamped a hand over the mouthpiece.

'Marianne! For Christ's sake! Stop that.'

She grinned wickedly.

'—Tim, I've been checking for you on that Godwin sideboard you said that one of the State galleries in Australia had bought.'

Marianne began to slide down the bed, pulling the sheet over her head, right next to me.

'For God's sake!' I hissed. 'Cut it out!'

'Tim, are you listening?'

'Yes, yes, of course. I'm all agog. Ahhh!'

She was right under now. Her hands moved over me.

'What?' Sue's voice was sharp.

'Nothing! Please go on!'

The blonde hair brushed my skin. I began to writhe.

'It took me a hell of a time, but I found what you wanted.'

I tried to turn away, but she pinned my legs down.

Squirming, I spoke to Sue. 'Oh good, good. Well—well done.'

'Have you got a paper and pen handy?'

'Yes, er, yes. Don't stop. Please. Don't stop. Go on.'

'They got the piece through a firm in San Francisco. It had its original William Watt invoice with it, dated eighteen-seventy-eight: Absolutely authentic, bought by a wealthy family in Oakland and shipped out from London.'

'My God.'

The sheets rustled as Marianne moved relentlessly.

'Well, really, I'm not quite sure what more you wanted. They wouldn't say how much they paid for it, but a friend of mine in the service reckoned it was sixty thousand dollars.'

I tried to reach down and push her off, but she was gaining ground.

'Tim?'

'Yes, I'm still here.'

'Your voice sounds sort of strangled.'

'It must be the line.'

'Odd. It wasn't to start with. Well, anyway, I had an awful job finding out what it was that I think you really wanted. I had to go out with the most foul little man—really poisonous—he seemed to think that giving me the information entitled him to do anything he liked.'

'An-Anything?'

'Yes, my God, you owe me back, really you do. He put his hand up my skirt, right up, I mean, in the restaurant I had to go to.'

'Christ.'

'Yes, imagine! I let him have it.'

'Have it. You did what?'

'Yes, of course! I slapped him, hard.'

'Hard?'

'He just laughed. Said he liked a sport. Then he told me.

It's supposed to be the most frightful secret. Never reveal their sources unless authorized, special concession, etcetera, etcetera, all that stuff. Would I go to Manley with him. No, I wouldn't I said. So he told me.'

'For God's sake, oh, for God's sake—'

'All right, all right, I'm coming to it. Just you remember, though, what it cost me. He said that the official documents were all in the name of some export shippers, Pacific Art Packers or something like that. They handled all the invoices and things. But the real sellers were a San Francisco firm of dealers, very low profile apparently, not usually in this sort of thing, Apple something—you know the States, everything's the Big Apple or whatever now, even computers—here it is, Applemore. Applemore Antiques.'

Dead silence. Only the soft rustling under the bedclothes. Simpson frozen, holding the phone.

'Are you there? Tim?'

Paralysis. My mouth suddenly arid, arms and legs congealed with dreadful fear. Eventually, five aged seconds later, I managed a croak.

'Yes I'm here. I've got it. Thanks. I mean, thanks very much. Terrific. More than enough.'

'I should think so! Well, I can't hang about. This is costing a fortune. Bye-bye, Tim, sweetheart. Be good.'

'I will. 'Bye. Oh God, goodbye.'

Click. I put the phone down.

Marianne's tousled fair head came out from under the sheet, mouth still grinning wickedly but blue eyes looking concerned.

'What's the matter, Tim? You've gone all tense again, d'you know that?'

CHAPTER 18

Earls Court Square does not only have theatrical and cultural associations for me. I lived there once, like almost all the London-based graduates of my generation and those before me. Countless thousands of British adult hopefuls were there before Max Wilson brought the South Africans to the Overseas Visitors Club, and the South Africans were there and made it partly theirs years before the Australians arrived. Earls Court street plans are engraved like maps in the minds of thousands of young starters who had their first jobs in London. When the Aussies came in, people started to call it New South Kensington; it was much more subtle than the coarse epithet of Kangaroo Valley, but subtlety is not an Australian quality.

I remembered clearly the alley down the side of Wetherton Mansions, where rusting blow-pipes still cling to the side of the building, left over from the days when the kitchens of each flat, in vertical succession, could be called up on these naval-style blowers. A puff to the mouthpiece in the alley at the bottom made a whistle blow at the top end. It saved a lot of tedious stair-climbing for the cooks and kitchen staff and much more for the tradesmen who called on them, since there were no lifts in those heavy, red-brick London mansions. Once, years ago, I tried to use a blow-pipe to save myself the climb to the kitchen of a girlfriend, to see if she was at home. I remembered that the whistle was still in place at the top end of the pipe, in her kitchen. I placed my mouth to the blower-piece, filled my lungs, and blew. The whistle went all right; I heard it, floors above me; my mouth filled with a great shower of rust-flakes that poured down the pipe and left me spluttering among the dustbins.

It was dark. For the whole afternoon and early evening I had sat alone in the Fulham Road, thinking and wondering what the hell to do. Marianne left at lunch-time, saying that Tony was expecting her to go with him to a Sunday market somewhere, looking for smalls. She didn't seem to notice my preoccupation as anything more than my normal tendency to ponder, but I caught her glancing at me thoughtfully from time to time, and when she picked up her handbag, before she snapped her mirror-powder-compact back into it, she paused, in tension, for a moment. The male nervous system, if reasonably healthy, is capable of absorbing quite a range of shocks before it is affected too drastically in sexual performance and I had acquitted myself with competence, feeling, as she clung to me with what seemed like genuine affection, that I had got into a hell of a mess.

I couldn't believe that she was involved. It just wasn't possible. It had to be Applemore himself in some way. No flicker of recognition had passed her face at Ellen Terry's house, no querying of my search for a sideboard. Yet Tony Applemore had sold a genuine Godwin sideboard; Peter had visited Belgy; Applemore had visited Belgy; both Peter and Belgy were dead, murdered. Why?

The cast-iron fire-escape at the back of the mansions was filthy, greasy with soot and rust. I swung on to it with a mild squeak, but it was solid under the dirt. Don't ask me why I didn't go straight up to their rented flat on the third floor, ring the bell and confront Applemore. I just didn't; I wasn't sure of myself. Perhaps some sort of early Boy Scout or cadet training, lost in my subconscious self, warned me to reconnoitre first. The fire-escape goes up to back bedroom windows mostly, with stops at occasional other exits. It used to be a way of creeping up to girlfriends' bedrooms, where they would let you in, surreptitiously raising the sash, so that their girl flatmates or guardian relatives didn't know that they had a boyfriend in for the night.

Quite like old times it was, creeping up the dirty grilled treads with a tingle of fear, on a cold dark night, like a criminal on the prowl. Up past lighted but curtained windows, up past one or two uncurtained, so that I had to time my crossing, a quick flash in the bright light while no one was in the room. Once, with a window illuminating a half-flight of stairs all the time, I really felt exposed, but for the rest of it I was lucky. Quite unexpectedly I knew I had arrived at the third floor level, knees shaking, breath gasping, heart jerking so unsteadily that I leant, for a moment, against the rough, porous brick surface to calm myself. The window was a plain big London sash with shiny, flaking white paint. The curtains were almost closed, but not quite enough to prevent my seeing in. I wish now that they had been; times are when blocked vision can be a blessing.

The room was well-lit, a bedroom, with a double bed and a chest of drawers and two chairs. Against the wall stood a suitcase, labelled, and a smaller grip sagged emptily beside it on the dark red carpet. The room was empty. I shifted my weight and glanced outwards, suddenly aware of the height, the black drop below my feet and the cold April wind at the upper reaches of the building. My breath was still unsteady, my knees were still weak and I was thinking of sitting on the stone window-sill for a moment to rest when Marianne came into the room.

She'd been having a bath. A white towel was wound round her head like a turban, covering her hair, and a white bathrobe was drawn round her. She stood for a moment in front of a wall mirror, arms raised, rubbing the towel into the wet hair beneath it. Then she laughed. I couldn't hear the sound of it, I just saw her face crack open into a rich grin and the white teeth flash in the mirror as she turned to talk to Tony Applemore, who had just come into the room.

A bit intimate, that, but I suppose a partner with his particular inclinations would be more like a close girlfriend than anything else. He was still wearing his jeans, but not his jacket, just a T-shirt, and he was in his socks. Very casual, like someone would be who has come back from a long drive and wants to get the old feet aired a bit. She laughed again and he stood talking, gesticulating a bit and shoving his hip sideways as he transferred his weight to one leg, as queers often do, posing for effect. She laughed again and stopped massaging the towel-turban into her head, so that she could step across and kiss him.

No, not on the cheek. On the lips.

That couldn't possibly be right. It couldn't be. He didn't pull back. He put his arms around her, pulling her closer, kissing her again. Then, quite casually, he pulled the bath-robe off her shoulders, downwards, kissing her on the side of her neck. She stood back, her face suddenly intent, and let the robe fall to the floor so that she stood naked in front of him. That couldn't be right. Then she was pulled to him again, so that the fabulous body was pressed up to him, but I must be seeing wrongly, he couldn't be sliding his hands down her body like that, he couldn't be. And now, no, that was wrong, she couldn't be helping him off with jeans, she couldn't be, but she was, and now they were on the bed and he was between her knees, he couldn't be, he couldn't be, they couldn't be doing that, they couldn't be . . .

But they were. Dear bloody God, they were.

On the corner of the Earls Court Road there was a lamp-post and I leant up against it for support while I vomited, knees shaking, ague-ridden stomach cramping, my clothes dirty and streaked where I'd run, as quietly but as fast as I dared, back down the horrid fire-escape in the foul cold April night, crashing down the alley where I stumbled between the dustbins into the bright glare of the street and the traffic.

Presently, behind me, stood the policeman, that same policeman, without his bluebottle bird this time, and he recognized me, and did a mock-jovial Jack Warner bit as he watched, saying hello hello hello what have we 'ere, sir, not again, am I to expect that there is another cadaver in the offing or what, it's Mr Simpson isn't it and no mistake . .

That policeman was lucky. If I hadn't been so sick and spin-brained, shaking and weak, I would have smashed him to the pavement, into the cracks, like a squashed snail.

CHAPTER 19

The blow that George Jackson had given to the back of my head was spreading a huge pain structure through my skull as I lay on the floor of Belgy's antique furniture warehouse. One eye, the right one, was transfixed by an iron spike of sharp agony. The floor was not too hard, but it was hot, burning hot, and I kept shifting my head to press an area of skin on to a cooler surface for relief. Cramp spread through one leg.

They were hammering on the floor beside me to release a tangled pile of smashed furniture in which Belgy was trapped. His booted leg stuck out from under a chest, like the witch's did from under a house at the end of the film of *The Wizard of Oz*. His phone kept ringing, intermittently, until the answering machine cut it off. I felt very ill, not the sort of passing illness, like 'flu, that you smile about tolerantly and laugh off, but stricken, spavined, permanently damaged, terminal.

I remembered leaving the policeman's luminous, humorous face in rage and walking stiffly into The Bolton Arms on the corner, where I must have drunk until closing time. I brought a bottle out with me. I couldn't remember whether it was a half or a full bottle but it didn't matter, because I fell down twice in Redcliffe Gardens, walking home, and the second time the bottle smashed, coursing rivulets of whisky into the cracks between the paving stones. No one helped me to get up.

My leg cramp got worse and I tried to move, finding that my trousers had bunched into the groin and cut the blood supply off, so it wasn't surprising. Odd, that, the trousers being in the way, because I was in bed. No, I wasn't, I was on it. I don't know how I got there.

There was an empty bottle of cherry brandy on the floor, against the skirting-board. It must have come from the kitchen. Dreadful stuff, sweet, sticky, for use at Christmas. I couldn't move my arm. I was lying on it. The noise of the traffic was intrusive, rasping, persecuting my ears. I wasn't in Hastings, I was at home, still half-tight, with a hangover like the Hindenburg. It was very bright. I tried opening the left eye, which was pretty bad. The right one was unusable. Thunder and ringing started again. It was at the door, so I rolled over, got up, hit the wall, focus gone, walked to the bedroom door, hit the jamb, swore, staggered across the living-room and opened up.

'Jesus God,' said Nobby Roberts.

The light was blinding.

'Either piss off or come in,' I said.

He came in and I closed the merciful door to shut the light out before I sat down on the edge of the burst sofa.

'I think I'm going to be sick,' I said thoughtfully.

'Then for Christ's sake get to the bogs,' he snapped. 'You—you—no, I'm not going to say it. Dear God, Tim, what the hell have you been at?'

The room revolved and stopped, temporarily. My stomach gave a dreadful, hollow groan.

'It's all right. I'm not going to be sick now. Not until I have breakfast.'

He put a hand to the side of his head and wiped his face before he spoke.

'Bloody stroll on. I went to South Ken station this morning and I bumped into one of the uniformed branch who told me that my friend has been seen heaving up into the gutter again, Earls Court way. So I ask what the hell they meant and they told me that it's that Mr Simpson what found the Blackwell body, ain't it. Earls Court Road but we think he was just half seas over if you know what we mean, nudge nudge wink wink. No corpse this time that could be seen anywhere except perhaps Mr Simpson himself, looked terrible, our man said.

'So when I'd finished my business at the station—which I'll come to in a minute because it's important—I phone your office and they haven't seen you like for days, so I think I'll drop in to see what's what and this is it, is it, the great freedom of bachelor life? Jesus, Tim, look at you, I must say you're in great shape for a funeral or something—'

'Cut it out.'

I went past him into the kitchen and put a kettle on. It wasn't easy but I did it. When the water boiled I made two mugs of coffee and a bowl of instant porridge with maple syrup and skimmed milk on it. He sipped his coffee while he watched me eat it.

'Will that stay down?' he inquired anxiously.

I grunted. 'It usually does. Lines the stomach and gets thing moving inside. It all depends—it might not.'

I drank the coffee. The right eye was now usable but painful. Four aspirins went down on top of the porridge to help that problem. Blood, stationary until now, started to move slowly through my veins, bringing a warmer feeling and a genuine, unhealthy flush to my cheeks. A shower, shave and change of clothes made me feel slightly more improved. When I got back into the living-room he had made some more coffee, found a loaf of bread, two sausages and some bacon, which he had grilled. We ate the sausages and bacon between hunks of the bread.

'Lunch,' he said cheerfully. 'Quite like old times, isn't it?'

I looked at him with suspicion. 'Why are you being so nice to me?'

He stopped eating for a moment and looked at me a bit sheepishly.

'I've got some news.'

'So have I.'

'You first.'

His clear, fit face looked at me expectantly as he dusted crumbs off himself, brushing them off his lap as he had that day at Jeremy's office, on to the armchair and thence to the carpeted floor. His frame was alert; his sharp eyes watched me, waiting brightly for my story, like the expectation of a cleanly-passed ball from a reliable inside three-quarter capable of performing, at least, certain basic skills to a reasonable standard. Why did Nobby always make me feel a sense of responsibility and guilt? Lucky Nobby, his eyes fixed on some far-distant touchline of ambition, untrammelled by passion or distorting physical desires, using his professional training to assess what I was about to tell him objectively, calmly, seeming to be uninvolved with the errant friend who was harassed by weakness and desire. For a moment I hesitated, resenting him, reluctant to plunge into the telling of a story that wouldn't be easy, even for a man less involved than I was. But he anticipated me, his expression softening in understanding and, surprisingly, his voice apologetic in tone as he said, 'Come on, Tim, out with it. There's an apology coming to you from me and the boys, but not until I've heard your side first.'

So, that making it easier, I started, from the day she came into my office in Park Lane to the diversion at Small Hythe and Wittersham, then on to the frightening, hateful, degrading view from the fire-escape at Wetherton Mansions. I didn't give him every detail, it was unnecessary, but I told him of Sue's research and information from Australia, the deception that exposed the stupid mug sitting in front of him, hating himself and everything connected with the whole horrid story. His expression, as each stage of the affair unfolded, changed from alert attention to amazement, deeper comprehension and, finally, to one of great sympathy. When I had finished he waited for a moment, staring at the floor, then he looked up.

'My news is different,' he said.

'Fire away.' It was a relief to have finished and to be waiting for his turn.

'We've done our forensic work.' He was intent on holding my attention, making sure that he presented himself to me in some way that he must have thought out previously. 'There's no doubt that Peter Blackwell and Klooster were killed with the same gun. It's a .32 calibre hand gun, quite small, well, quite small compared to a police .38, say, but no doubt of any sort. It means that their murders are linked, the mutual involvement is certainly implicit and that your instinct was probably right. We've no idea, yet, what it was all about but we certainly owe you an apology. Unreservedly. George Jackson was very emphatic that I should lay it on for you. In some way or another, you were right; maybe for the wrong reasons and you've been a bloody awkward squad, but there it is. I should have known—and remembered—you better. I'm sorry.'

He made me feel much worse. Much, much worse. I mean, I had behaved towards him like a bear with a sore head, well I did have a sore head, I suppose, and had been churlish and insulting and resentful of his every sterling virtue. Yet here he was, and I knew it couldn't have been easy for him, apologizing with the grace and sincerity of an early Christian saint. I felt like a real, prize, chromium-plated turd.

'For Heaven's sake, Nobby,' I muttered somehow, 'I could easily have been wrong. It was all pure speculation, you know. Thanks anyway and my apologies in return for being such a bloody nuisance. Say no more?'

He grinned cheerfully. 'Say no more, Tim. Let's forget that and decide on the next move. From what you've told me it should be pretty clear.'

It was an enormous relief to be justified, but my heart was still too sore to take any satisfaction in Nobby's news. I sat glumly, irresolute, in the cheerless vindication of my obstinate pursuit, my hopes in ruins, with a monstrous hangover.

'Well I don't know,' I answered him. 'It was all a con, wasn't it? On me, I mean.'

His eyes dropped to the worn patch on the carpet where my feet usually rest while I'm watching the telly.

'It seems like it.'

'For God's sake say yes or no! Why did she pretend that Applemore is a queer? Even the timing, that day she called at the office, was so cleverly done, so that one thing could lead to another and I'd think what a clever, attractive, seductive laddie I was. Why gloss over any inquiry about Godwin, no curiosity about the sideboard I was looking for, when all the time she knew that Applemore had sold one to Australia?'

'Perhaps she didn't—'

'She must have! She's sleeping with him, she's his girl-friend! All this time. All this time that I thought that he—she—'

'Tim, stop it. You've gone and got yourself terribly involved, you can't see it straight. She might just be a promiscuous type.'

'The bullets, Nobby, the bullets! They link Peter and Belgy Klooster. Klooster and Applemore are linked. She and Applemore are staying only a stone's throw from Peter's shop. What more do you want?'

'Hell hath no fury like a Simpson deceived.' He looked at his watch. 'We'd better move. There's certainly enough to justify questioning them, even if it isn't yet quite as clear-cut as you would like to believe. I'd better take some precautions, though, and I don't like it, but you'd better come too. At least I can keep an eye on you for a bit.'

He downed the rest of his coffee, wiped some bacon fat off his mouth with a blue handkerchief, and stood up. 'Where to, then?'

'Third floor, Wetherton Mansions.'

'Right. I'll make a call from the car. Outside, on the yellow lines. Off we go.'

We clattered down into the bright cold sunlight. The blast of traffic in full spate hit me and I stopped, transfixed, as we reached the kerb.

'There's something else, you know,' I said.

He paused at the door of the car, key in hand. 'What?'

'It's not called *The Letter*. Sorry, just a stupid thought that suddenly hit me.'

'What isn't? What are you talking about?'

'Orpen's painting. It's not called *The Letter*. I've just remembered. It's called *The Disappointing Letter*.'

He didn't say anything. He just gave me a strange, uncomprehending look and he got in the car. All the way up Finborough Road he talked into a microphone until we reached Warwick Road and turned into Earls Court Square from the west side.

We stood outside the thick front door of the old mansion flat on the third floor, ringing the bell until we were joined by two men, serious-faced, who nodded at Nobby and looked hard at me, as though they would have liked to finger my collar, until Nobby told them that I was on the right side, so they relaxed a bit and nodded to me too, looking about as friendly as those Alsatian dogs do, provided that you don't pat them. One of the two hard men was taking out a bunch of keys when a door opened up the passage and an old bird came out in carpet slippers, carrying a rubbish bin with a broken pedal top. She stopped when she saw us.

'Gone, haven't they,' she said triumphantly.

One of Nobby's men smiled, like a leaded paned window reflecting a leaded sky. 'Who, dear?' he asked.

'The American couple. Service flats, these are. I do for 'em. Thought they was staying longer, but they left, din't they, round tennish, bag and baggage. They was all paid up so it din't make no difference. Off back to America they said. In a taxi.'

I looked at my watch. It made the right eye hurt again, but it was good to know that it worked.

'It's half past one' I said. 'Most of the flights to the States leave between eleven and three. You might just catch them.'

By the time I had walked, slowly, down the three flights of stairs on my own and out on to the pavement, the other two had gone, but Nobby was sitting behind the wheel of his car, talking away into his little blower.

'They're checking the passenger lists,' he grated irritably. 'All of them. It's a quick job now, with computers.'

I nodded. 'If they're working. Don't forget Gatwick. They might fly to Atlanta or somewhere like that and connect onwards.'

And it's on the way to Brighton too, I thought irrelevantly. My eye was throbbing badly. The bright sunlight glanced through the plane trees, still only sprinkled with their green spring sprouts. Nobby snapped off his set.

'Pan American,' he snarled furiously. 'New York and San Francisco. Booked yesterday. Left at one o'clock. Shit. Bugger. Damn. Blast.'

'Language, Nobby,' I murmured as I walked away slowly down the pavement. 'It's not like you to go on like that.' A feeling of tremendous relief was sweeping through me as I realized that what was left to be done could be done without the complications I had dreaded handling, for emotional reasons.

But Nobby shouted after me as I walked away. 'Hey! Where are you going?'

'To The Bolton Arms. Come on, I need a pint, urgently, and so do you.'

After that, there was only one place to go.

CHAPTER 20

Nobby parked carefully, near the station. He got out and stared at me.

'I don't like it,' he said, 'but at least we're both quite clear, are we?'

'I am. Bloody sure you are.'

He nodded. 'You go ahead, then. I'll follow. There's something more I need, in the car.'

'OK. Don't be long.'

'I won't. Be careful, Tim. Remember what we've agreed.'

'Bollocks.' I grinned at him, to show that it wasn't serious.

Sea air is clear. The light at the seaside, as any painter will tell you, is much purer than inland, making the houses and objects stand out at your vision like an aggressive 3D card. I squinted and scowled to keep the light out. You couldn't see the minareted domes of that effeminate idiot's Pavilion, nor the elegant façades along the promenade, between the piers, where they have buggered up the whole aspect by planting down modern blocks with blank walls twelve feet high, like Yankee factories, right in the middle. None of that.

The back streets of Brighton are mean, like any other gridiron of jerry-built workers' terraces. Cheap junk shops and ex-Service surplus gear; second-hand kitchenware; so-called art traders, desperate runners in criminal vans, and high-blown fences in Rollers; that's the back of Brighton. Fourth street, half way along, a big shopfront with a side driveway leading to a warehouse, the Luton with the blue square patch repairing its back corner standing outside, still there, the way it was that first day, called me to attention. The furniture was still piled up to the windows, grilled with wire mesh. One notice said Trade and Export Only; the other said Closed. I pressed down the door handle, put my shoulder to the door, and shoved. Nothing doing. Standing back, I lunged at it, pressing the handle down as I hit. There was a splintering noise and I fell through. My luck was in; no mortice locks on.

The lad inside came out from behind the pedestal desk, showing off the tattoos on his brawny arms.

''Ere,' he shouted, 'wot the fuckin' 'ell are you doin'?'

'Where's Meeson?'

He glanced back towards the far end of the shop, giving it all away. Just a boy, you see.

'He's out. You can't break in like that. I'll—'

'Push off, sonny.'

He was quite a big lad, his tattoos just like the ones that Belgy's boys had, used to carrying heavy loads, and strong, but slow in his strength. The muscles you need for violence were half-developed and I put him at about nineteen. I used to fancy myself at that age too, but now I know; there's still an inevitable softness there, something young, lacking stamina, good for athletic work but not really hard, nasty, like an older man. He swung a right at me, easily sidestepped, and I kicked his back heel out from under him, hooking him hard in the face as he went down. His head jerked and he crumpled on the floor, blood seeping from one nostril and an involuntary tear of pain and shock blinking in the corner of one eye. Poor stupid kid.

Down the aisles of furniture, towards the back, light gleamed under a door. I was three-quarters of the way down, moving fast towards it, when the dirty-pullover professional stepped out from behind a bookcase and hit me, hard, on the side of the jaw, so that my head snapped back and I tripped, going over heavily to the floor.

He jumped after me, bringing his right foot down with all his weight, aimed at my crutch, but I had already rolled to keep out of the ruck and he hit my hip instead. The heavy shoe ground across and stamped the floor, where I grabbed it with both hands and twisted.

He had to come round; I've seen it in scrums before. Either he came round or I would break his foot, snapping the bones at the ankle and leaving the foot sticking out the wrong way. He tried to stoop to hit me or to shift his weight, using the other leg, but you can't do that while someone is twisting your foot off. He had to come round, until he was the wrong way, back to me, facing into a flat high stack of furniture. I got one foot underneath me, put my weight on to my legs doubled under me, and then, letting go the foot, stood up, shoving my shoulder under his buttocks and into his fork so that I lifted him, high, into the air.

I got one hand into his crutch and used the arm to lift him higher, crunching him into my fist so that he shrieked and turned, trying to hit at my head. He was too high to do any real damage, he just angered me more as he clipped the place where George Jackson had clubbed me, bringing tears to my eyes. I tightened my grip and got my other hand clamped behind his knee, ready for a throw.

He gave one more shriek and grabbed the nearest thing to him with both hands, finding the big wooden turned knobs on the drawer of a chest at the top of the pile. The drawer pulled half out, so I let him go and stood back, out of the way.

For a moment the silly bugger hung, instead of letting go and falling to his feet. Then the whole chest tipped over and fell down on him as he landed under it, hitting his head and splitting the top corner as it crashed to the floor. I hit him very hard on the jaw. He was on the deck but he was still moving, ready for action, so I kicked him in the kidneys. I know; it's not very nice; I'm not proud of it, but I was in a hurry and I couldn't afford to take any more risks. He stiffened, arching backwards with his jawbone stretching open. A croak like a stuck frog came out of him and he stayed rigid, like an epileptic, hands clapped to his back. The tattooed lad took one look and scarpered through the broken front door. Sensible kid.

The door at the end gave on to a passage. The passage opened into a warehouse. On the right-hand side, partitioned off, were the workshops. The warehouse was full of furniture but devoid of human life. I walked across it, found a door and jerked it open. As I stepped into the long professional workshop, with its benches and racks of tools, the smell of varnish, white spirit, meths, acetone and shavings all struck my nostrils. A familiar, normally happy smell, of human skill and endeavour.

Not this time.

She was standing at the far end, wearing the linen suit and the white blouse that I remembered from Park Lane, Sutton Valence and Small Hythe. The shock of seeing her froze me to the spot. She should have been well past mid-Atlantic by now. As if that shock were not enough, my eye took in the contents of the flat cardboard packs carefully stacked against one wall, the red shiny hardwood gleaming in the light. The lower half of one sideboard was already assembled in the centre of the floor in raw mahogany-style Korean finish. The other sideboard was at the far end, near her, already complete and ebonized jet black. Someone had started to fix the silver-plated hinges and fittings to it.

She turned to look at me.

'The black buffet,' I said, breaking the spell. 'That's what you call them, isn't it? That was what was on the invoice wasn't it, the original one from William Watt. A black buffet. What were you going to do? Sell them in pairs? Turn them out wholesale?'

Her expression didn't change. Behind her, against the wall, was a big breakfront wardrobe they were going to convert into a Georgian bookcase and someone had leant a sheet of old picture glass against it, ready to put in the doors when they were made. In it, reflected, I could see Meeson as he crouched behind a wardrobe to my right, swinging the big, heavy steel sash cramp down at my head.

Even though I jumped, swinging sideways and downwards, the metal end of the cramp caught my shoulder and tore my tweed jacket right down the front, pulling away a great flap of material. The swing overbalanced him forwards a lot, so that his head was towards me and I hit it, three times, left, right, left, before he straightened and I really went to work on him, intent on smashing him to a pulp.

'Stop that!' she shouted.

The gun was in her hand. I let Meeson slide to the floor, too far gone to matter. Shock and distress paralysed me again; my last stupid hope had been scuppered by the sight of that gun in her hand, because it was smallish, like you would expect a .32 to be.

'It was you all the time.' My voice sounded far away.

She said nothing. She had become a terrible, menacing figure.

'Why? For God's sake, why?'

The linen suit was still flawless, even in those surroundings. Hardly a crease. 'Look at that junk out there. You ask me why?'

Apart from the shout, it was the first time she'd spoken. The voice was no different, it was the same voice, the one that had joked and laughed and whispered to me in bed, in the car, where else? I stood hopeless in disbelief, but I had to talk.

'You had one piece of luck. Just one, like every antique dealer is entitled to, now and again. The Godwin sideboard you sold to Australia. All that other line about the good pieces you'd handled that you spun in my office was codswallop. Wasn't it?'

'That's right! We had just one break, just one! And then what? The recession hit; that break paid off some rental and interest on our operation. And then? More years of grinding with this lousy junk or else getting into the grip of some greasy financier who'd scam all the profit and keep telling you that you're only as good as your last deal and want more and more. Not for me, Mr Tim Simpson, not for me.'

'Oh, come on! It doesn't have to be like that, and you know it.' I stepped towards her. 'Marianne! You could still—'

'Stop! Stop right there. You and your safe, comfortable job and someone else's finance to play with! I hate smug bastards like you.'

It hadn't meant anything. She'd never thought anything of me at all, just playing for survival, whoring for safety.

'Tony. Your partner. He left for San Francisco today all right, didn't he? You pretended to go too. I was banking on your being gone. Why didn't you? Oh, why didn't you? Tony was the—he was your—'

'Lover, yes. Tony is a real man. A lot of our business is with gays, they like to deal with each other, like Jews, as I told you. He was good at mingling with them, making like them. But Tony was never any gay, he's a real lover, not some clumsy football oaf, he knows how to please, he's got narrow hips, he isn't a great lousy bull. I really need Tony and I split the operation with him, but it's always been mine, so he drew off the fire by going on the plane while I thought I'd get on and finish off the last details here, but you—you—I should have known—'

'Stop it, Marianne! There's no need—'

'Stay back, I said! I told you to say back!' She brought up the gun. She was serious; I knew absolutely, now, that she was as serious with me as she had been with Peter and Belgy. My insides congealed. Where the hell was Nobby?

'Why me? Why?'

'Snooper, that's you, snooping around. What was it that

you said you were before White picked you up? A business consultant, another kind of snooper.' Her mouth twisted in dislike. 'Other people's business, that's you. You can't stay away from it, can you? I should have dealt with you at your flat when I found out that you had no ties, no one to butt in, just your own miserable selfish life. But it was kind of a new experience, you know, you were kind of interesting and naive. I thought I might even sell you a sideboard one day, indirectly, and I didn't like to think of myself as like a spider or a queen bee after copulation, you know what I mean?' Her eyes held mine strongly for a moment, and a wild hope that some other element, some other emotion was in them gripped me for a brief second, but they suddenly turned cold. 'There's one consolation,' she went on, bitterly and hard, 'you don't believe that you'll have to sit there waiting for me, do you? It might have been better for you if you did.'

'So that was the trouble in the church at Small Hythe. Peter's ghost. That was what was worrying you. And I laid it for you, let you out of worrying about it. Cleared the way for you to deal with Belgy, did't?'

Her face froze. She glanced over my shoulder as Nobby's shoe crunched on the shavings strewn on the floor. I sensed rather than heard the spang as she pulled the trigger and the gun jumped. It is when the dentist jabs the end of the needle loaded with novocaine into the gum that the pain is felt, not afterwards, as the gentle numbness spreads. His face was white, dead white, and his eyes hollow as he shouted the words every police officer has to shout, despite the odds.

'I am a police officer! I am armed! Freeze! Armed police! Freeze!'

'Nobby! Don't!'

Spang. Another prick, more serious this time, deeper, pushing me backwards as he braced himself, the police .38 big in his hands as he crouched, his face etched with dreadful tension as he realized what he was going to have to do.

'Oh no! Please, Nobby! Don't do it!'

But now the numbness was spreading further and I seemed to be falling as the two terrible bangs drowned my shout. I saw her, silently, going over backwards with two terrible red marks on the crisp blouse. As she checked, half-caught by the bench behind her, the skirt rode up over her knees like it had that day in the car, on the old sea cliffs overlooking the marsh and the Channel. Then she crumpled, out of sight.

Darkness was spreading as well as numbness now, all quite painlessly and unreally, so that it didn't seem strange when George Jackson stepped out into the light and ran towards me. Another man I didn't recognize came up beside Nobby and held out an open polythene bag, nodding into his stricken face so that, quite automatically, Nobby dropped the revolver into the bag and the man closed it as he stared, horrified, in my direction. Some other men came in and started to walk quite quickly round the benches towards the place where she had been standing as it went completely dark.

CHAPTER 21

The senior physician was a large, dreadfully cheerful bastard who'd played for St Mary's Hospital in the late Fifties. He seemed to think that I was a contemporary, which shows how aged I must have looked. He was standing now at the foot of the bed with a gaggle of sycophantic students in white coats who goggled at me obediently.

'Here, ladies and gentlemen,' he boomed, trying evidently to impress the females that he was no male chauvinist, which he was, but still . . . 'we have a patient who comes to us as a result of mixing with members of the criminal classes and the antique trade. If that is not a tautology, ha, ha.'

The prospective medical professionals all sniggered obligingly. If they knew what the antique trade says about doctors in return, they might have reacted even more. Many a choice piece has been gratefully passed on to the doctor in the will of a dying widow, to the fury of the local dealers.

'Fortunately for his own sake,' he boomed on, 'the patient is possessed of a remarkably thick set of ribs. Something which some of you here—' he looked contemptuously at the weedy bunch of blokes around him—' might well have done with. That is, of course, if you'd had any interest in any masculine sort of sport.'

The girls tittered and he went on, flattered.

'The first bullet—' he was enjoying himself, he can't have had that many shot patients—'glanced off the right side after hitting the central ribs and doing relatively little superficial damage of a minor nature.'

Relatively minor. It ached like buggery.

'The second, however, penetrated the ribcage, passing through—'

Penetrated. What he meant was that it smashed its way in, bloody near perforated a lung, severed various bits and pieces that are not meant to be severed and wound up in the back of the ribcage, from where a surgeon extracted it. A surgeon, mark you, not a physician. To hear the Mary's man talking, you'd think that he'd done it himself.

I felt dreadful and his talk started to blur in my ears as I let my wretched condition, mental and physical, overcome me. She was dead; Nobby killed her while she was trying to kill me. I'd had few visitors; George Jackson and some other Brighton policemen, then Jeremy, quite distraught and anxious, ahead of anyone else. You could rely on Jeremy to turn up when things were the way they were. He peered at me distractedly through tunnelled mists.

'Tim, I did ask you to try not to get involved. Really I did, you know. Don't you remember? And you got tangled up with this woman who was right in it. It really is appalling, I mean, you've been shot by her, for Heaven's sake. It's my fault too, of course. I'm afraid my enthusiasm for the Aesthetic Movement carried us both along. No, that's not fair: you were quite right really, but it does seem odd how everything connected with that crowd does seem to come to a bad end. I mean look at Wilde and—I say, are you all right?'

'Should have stuck to muscular, middle-class Christianity, eh, Jeremy?'

'Oh my God, Tim, I am so sorry, I must sound like an awful bore. It seems that you have uncovered a major attempt at fraud, I mean, faking Godwin furniture practically wholesale, dear Heavens, so Nobby Roberts told me before those grim-looking police commissioners or whatever they were took him off. And you uncovered the whole thing. Astounding. I'm dealing with tremendous inquiries from the press, whole story will be in the Sundays, makes the Art Fund once again the guardian of—in the forefront of—'

His face was sliding away from me.

'Tim? Tim? Are you listening? I say, Nurse, in here, in here at once, if you please—'

Bad nightmares followed; my fevered sleep in the hospital bed brought visions that stressed my ignorance and illusions, dreams that reiterated useless death-dates, like Godwin's in 1886, Ellen Terry's in 1928 and, unharmonious vibes now, Orpen's in 1931. The two men were each only 53 when they died; she was 81. In my dreams I kept trying, half-conscious, to shake Orpen off as irrelevant, immaterial to either Godwin or Terry, but somehow my nightmares mixed them all up, Godwin, Marianne, Orpen's painting of Yvonne, Earls Court mansions and houses, like a mad cocktail of unsuitable spirits that some poor party joker tries to pass off as a new, exciting mixture, only to know from the face of a taster that the components are not miscible. Then another death-date would intervene: Orpen's Yvonne, in 1973. Mad, Chinese arithmetic; Ellen Terry died 42 years after her lover Godwin; Yvonne died 42 years after her lover Orpen. Both men were 53 at their deaths; on it went, repetitive, stupid, numerate coincidence, the sort of thing that men imprisoned by walls or emotions keep churning round in their minds, trying to grasp a significant truth, a matching of equations, from the endless fruitless combinations. Nothing would come, nothing would help; I was an intruder, butting clumsily in to a world of overlapping lives that might or might not have been aware of each other—did Orpen see Ellen Terry at the theatre? Might I have passed Yvonne in the street? I had been ill, really ill, I told myself, on waking bathed in sweat, near death, I must stop this, try to forget it, as if I could convince myself that the past could ever be forgotten. I had only wanted a Godwin sideboard, not even for myself; what, at the end of the day, did I know about Godwin? Precious little: a little learning, a dangerous thing. Drink deep or taste not; that summed it up all right; deep drinking was going to be the order of the day when I got out of hospital.

'—the patient, eh?'

The St Mary's man was obviously asking me something. I looked at him, uncomprehending.

'How are you feeling today?' He repeated his question a bit louder, with slightly too professional a solicitude, concealing an irritation with someone either deaf or stupid but worthy of careful treatment in front of others. I felt my temperature rising.

'Pretty bloody.'

His face froze. The temperature fell. Patients are supposed to be humbly grateful and bootlicking, not truculent and disgruntled. For a moment there was an embarrassed silence, but since I wasn't looking at him, or indeed bothering to look particularly anywhere, I wasn't inclined to bother. My ribs hurt and I found breathing a bit better; that's all I noticed.

'I'm sorry to hear that.' The voice and manner had changed. I glanced at him and saw that he seemed genuinely concerned. The students were waved away, beyond some further bed behind the screened partitions and, when we were alone, he pulled up a chair and sat next to me.

'The patients who get better are the ones who want to,' he said, a little obviously.

'I know.'

'You're really very lucky. Injuries are quite minor, well, they may not feel like it, but for bullet wounds they're not bad and, from what I've heard, you're lucky to be alive. There's nothing that won't mend, physically, quite quickly. I can tell you that you'd probably feel a lot worse if you'd been tackled hard by MacSweeney.'

He smiled meaningly and I tried to think.

'Who? Oh, David MacSweeney, another doctor, Trinity Dublin and Cambridge, great thug of a bloke. Met him once. Before my time, played for Ireland, didn't he?'

He nodded. 'That's right.'

It was David MacSweeney who went on record as saying that wearing your light blue blazer to the Café Royal—why the Café Royal, I wondered, where the Wilde coterie used to meet—after the Twickenham match was all very fine if you'd beaten Oxford. You strutted about like peacock. If you'd lost, though, it made you feel like an ice-cream vendor.

I knew what he meant.

The Mary's man fiddled about a bit. 'Look, Tim, I hope you don't mind my calling you Tim, I saw you play so often and I feel I know you a bit more now, I realize that injuries to the soul take much longer to heal than the physical ones. There's been a policeman here on and off for some time, says he's a friend of yours. When they brought you in he was fussing about and then had to go away. He's here now. It's out of hours and breaks the rules, but if you want to see him, I'll send him up. How about it?'

Sweat broke out on my forehead. My ribs got hot and I felt queasy again. In my mind's eye I still could see that vision of Nobby, legs apart, gun clamped in his hands, shouting. I could see, even clearer, Marianne going over, the red splashes on her breast, the knees showing as they shouldn't have been to anyone else but me, stupid possessive thought, the thought of a man clinging to unreality. My feelings towards Nobby were very mixed but the moment had to be faced. Perhaps from then my real recovery could start.

I nodded. 'OK. I'd like that.'

'You're sure? I don't want you to be upset too early; I know what policemen are like.'

'It's all right. He is a friend. It'll help. Tell him to come up. Tell him—tell him to where I wait come gently on.'

'What?'

'Nothing. Just a phrase. And thanks.'

He looked satisfied but he held up a warning finger.

'You've still to be careful. Don't overdo it. I'll drop by a bit later to see how you are getting on.'

'Fair enough.'

Nobby looked older. I suppose many successful policemen have gone through worse moments of decision than Nobby's where life is involved and people get killed but not many, in Britain anyway, have to shoot a woman, and a damned pretty woman at that. His face was strained and his approach to my bedside was very cautious.

'Tim? How are you?'

'I'll last. And you?'

He sat down.

'Oh, I'm all right. I've tried to see you, but either you were blotto or I had the official inquirers standing on my toes and demanding to know what the hell I thought I was doing. They've put me through it, I can tell you.'

'Come on, Nobby. I expect they'll give you a lot of Brownie points or something.'

He shot me a glance.

'Don't do that, Tim. It's not the real you. I'm going to be credited with solving two murders and a major fraud, but risking your life by letting you go in first has been a bit hard to explain.'

'Sorry. I shouldn't have insisted, but you know how it was—it seemed like a good idea at the time. It was my involvement, not yours, and I wanted to be sure.'

He wiped his hands on his blue handkerchief.

'Look, I'm sorry, I really am. It was the worst thing that's ever happened to me. She was killing you in front of me; there was no other way of stopping her. I was too bloody slow as it was. I keep reproaching myself for that.'

'Well, you shouldn't. English policemen aren't supposed to pepper away as though they were in Chicago, are they? You did save my life. You're right, she was killing me, or would have. Pity she didn't.'

He wiped his hands some more, glaring at the floor.

'Don't be bloody silly, Tim.'

'Do you know what it was all about?'

'More or less, but not completely. Can you tell me? I mean, I don't want you to overdo it, the doc said—'

'Balls. She and Tony Applemore fell over a Godwin sideboard, a real one, in Oakland, California. They sold it, very low profile, to an Australian museum for sixty thousand dollars, a lot of money compared to the junk they were dealing in. It set them thinking. Their junk was all rubbish but some of it was just as well made. They copied the Godwin piece somehow, probably photographing it from every angle and drawing it, with all the measurements. At the same time, in that end of the trade, they saw all the stuff that is being made in Korea, either in their travels when they called on Belgy or even in the States itself. I guess it was through

Belgy, who'd got all the contacts and suggested they import the parts, to their design, from Korea in CKD form.'

'CKD?'

'Components Knocked Down. It's a standard way of shipping new furniture, to save space and cost. You assemble the pieces on arrival. The flat cardboard packaging I saw at Belgy's and in Meeson's Luton was what the parts were packed in. Coming from Korea, looking Oriental, in that mahogany, no one would even raise an eyebrow. Belgy was doing all sorts of repro from Korea, so he imported it along with the rest, and he probably knew the cheapest places to go to have it made. Meeson and his mob in Brighton assembled it, ebonized it and would have shipped it out to the States.'

'Why so long a chain? Why not bring it straight in?'

'Two reasons, I think. One would be provenance. UK origin to justify its authenticity. Came in with shipping goods in a container. House clearance gear. How the hell could anyone trace it back? All they had to do was to show that it came out from England with a load of other stuff. People—collectors especially—are greedy. They almost want to be fooled. Another aspect: the sideboard Applemore and Marianne sold to Australia had original William Watt invoices with it. I bet they copied them. All they had to do was to print on old paper, put in spurious addresses—Hastings, anywhere—and stuff them in a drawer to be "found" on arrival.'

'Surely all that could be checked?'

'Have you ever studied the Keating business? Eh? Art fraud policeman that you are?'

'Of course.'

'Do you seriously believe that his fakes look like real Samuel Palmer paintings, with their accompanying "documents" and all?'

'No.'

'Then how the hell did he or the dealers who tried to

handle his work get away with it for so long? I'll tell you—greed. People want to make those sorts of finds and they're prepared to swallow all sorts of codswallop to justify them. Those sideboards, suitably aged and faked, with invoices to match, would easily pass for quite a while, especially in America. You see, I've thought quite a lot about that. There's no problem in faking the mahogany—half the so-called Georgian mahogany you see in the shops nowadays has been reconstructed in some way and aged up with black wax—and there is no difficulty in giving a newly-ebonized surface some "age" by scratching it and toning it down with wire wool and stains, like watermark "rings" where someone is supposed to have left a glass or hot cup or something. That's maybe why they needed the Brighton connection; the Brighton boys have been duffing up lacquered surfaces for years.'

'But was it worth it? After all, how many could they do before the market got suspicious?'

'Ah, but that's the joy of it, Nobby! There were variants, small variations between one sideboard and another—two front legs, four front legs, a curtained cupboard instead of one with a door, and so on—that were easy to do with the do-it-yourself kits they imported. Half a dozen would be enough. Anywhere between three hundred thousand and half a million dollars if you worked it right, spread them about a bit, one to a museum, another to a dealer, another at auction, over a period, say a year or two, with careful organization, no problem to an experienced furniture shipper. All for an outlay of a few thousand; the Korean parts would cost only a song. The rest was shipping, assembly, ebonizing.'

'Then Peter Blackwell found them out?'

'Peter must have walked into Belgy Klooster's shop on just the wrong day. He probably only saw the doors and the frames out when Meeson and Klooster were looking at them but his mind was as sharp as a needle. He knew exactly what those parts would make. He came straight back and called me to meet him so he could tell me and show me his file on Godwin, to see the variants.'

'But she got there first?'

There was no other explanation. It had to be faced up to.

'They must have phoned from Hastings to tell her and Applemore. They gave her Peter's address. All she had to do was to walk round from Wetherton Mansions, possibly with Applemore, and wait. When he arrived home she or they followed him into the shop and, when she saw his gear, she knew that he must have cottoned on because he was obviously a specialist. She shot him and she—or they—rifled the shop to make it look like a break-in, almost Frisco style.'

Nobby shook his head slowly, in wonder.

'Then you arrived on the scene. And got involved.'

'Dead right. I got involved. They must have been nervous when I called on Belgy that day in Hastings, after the murder, asking about Peter. She—Marianne—decided to keep an eye on me, by—by getting as close as possible. Belgy became a liability because it was obvious that I wasn't satisfied and was going to keep after him until I got at the truth. As long as I was faffing about chasing red herrings like Small Hythe I was no problem, but getting close to Belgy might have blown the gaffe. She—she diverted me until they could deal with him; after all, he had a lot of loose connections who might have been after him and they really didn't need Belgy any more. They knew where the Korean parts came from and he was a liability; Meeson and his crowd were an uglier mob to deal with. It's funny, that; it's almost typical of the difference between Brighton and Hastings, you see. Small-time failure as against flash, violent success. Poor old Belgy. But by that time it was all getting much too complex and when I traced the Australian sideboard through Sue, I suppose I must have known the answer.' I looked at him, apologetically. 'I should have moved much earlier but—'

'But you were involved.'

'Yes.'

He grinned at me for the first time. 'It's understandable, Tim, and we didn't help, Jeremy and me, telling you to forget it and to lay off.'

'If she hadn't come to see me that day you were at the office, I might have let the whole thing drop.'

He shook his head. 'I doubt it. You're a tenacious bugger, Tim. I think that Applemore may have got away—it depends on the American police—but we've got the real culprits. I don't think he was so important.'

It was painful to think about that. I had no Godwin sideboard, no Marianne, nothing, and out there somewhere was Applemore, who might have answered many questions in my mind. She had proved to be as elusive for me as Godwin had been, as evanescent as a Tite Street interior and just as bankrupting, in her way. I had been a temporary diversion, rather in the same way that Godwin had been for Ellen Terry, though he thought differently at the time. Where would I go now?

As if reading my thoughts, Nobby spoke up.

'Tim, Gillian says you will come and stay with us to recuperate when you come out, won't you? She absolutely insists.'

'Oh, that's very kind, Nobby, but—'

The idea of Nobby's domesticity and his well-meaning, cheerful invitation to burden the pregnant Gillian's daily load, was not something that appealed, touched though I was. Either I would have to be alone, to go away somewhere distant, or I must try to pick up a workload again, soon, that would absorb me fully. Cooling my heels in someone else's happy household, like a spectre at the feast, was not my idea of recovery.

There was a flurry of steps and a blazered Jeremy suddenly appeared from behind the screens, like a large, well-tailored yachtsman with a briefcase in his hand. Nobby and I gaped at him in astonishment.

'Tim! Splendid! You're sitting up. They said that you ought to be better, so I thought I'd pop in on my way to the Hamble with a little suitable nourishment to celebrate your improvement and some superb publicity we've—no, no, you've—had about the sideboards. Everyone is absolutely agog. How nice to see you too, Inspector Roberts, or may I call you Nobby? I'm absolutely parched.'

He sat down on a chair that Nobby speechlessly indicated, glanced around him imperiously, opened the briefcase, and drew from it two bottles of champagne and a funnel of clear plastic beakers.

'Not terribly cold now, I'm afraid,' he said, cheerfully popping a cork with a blast that echoed like a pistol shot, 'but I do find that this attaché case does act as an insulant for up to two hours, so it shouldn't be too bad. The plastic beakers are horrible, I'll admit, but I always break any glasses I bring and the bits are so bad for invalids. They say this champagne is frightfully good for you; even my uncle always has a glass at about eleven or so. Here's to you both.'

Nobby gave me a quick wink as we toasted each other in silent admiration for Jeremy. I had forgotten the immediate lift that the sparkling liquid gives, and my obvious pleasure and surprise drew a great, delighted cadenza of laughter from Jeremy. Nobby started laughing too, so that the look of furious outrage on the returned senior physician's face as he suddenly and unexpectedly towered over us, congealed in amazement.

Jeremy greeted his appalled countenance with familiar spontaneity.

'Splendid! You've come to join us. I must congratulate

you, Doctor, he's looking far better. You will take a glass with us, won't you?'

The Mary's-trained eyes bulged. He opened his mouth to speak and then he caught sight, simultaneously, of the label on the bottle and of Nobby's face.

'Good God! That's a nineteen-seventy-one Moët! I certainly will. And you—Inspector—I've just realized where I've seen you before. Didn't you play on the wing for 'Quins a while back?'

Nobby lowered his eyes modestly as he took another draught from his beaker. 'Well, yes, on and off, but—'

'I knew it! I never forget a rugger face! Well, well, this is excellent. I don't suppose that Tim here—I see he's smiling a bit at last, thought he'd never cheer up—has told you that I played for—'

We hadn't the heart to stop him, yarning on about the big time rugby of the late Fifties, because he was so happy and it was his hospital, after all, and we could always talk later, whenever we liked. As he gossiped, Nobby and Jeremy joined in, stimulated by champagne, until they invited the ward sister—who suddenly looked like promising material—to join us too, and it started to become a party of sorts, with all of us slightly hysterical and exaggerated, as though we had just passed an enormous test of some sort for which our nerves had been strung to high tension and were now released. But then, as they talked of wings and hookers long forgotten to fame, my thoughts wandered to the old sea cliffs at Wittersham and to striped rugby socks on that lovely body in the early morning April sunlight in the Fulham Road. I thought, sadly, of the No. 30 bus, Putney to Hackney Wick, that goes past Drayton Gardens on its way, in dusty red dignity, towards the Victoria and Albert Museum en route to Park Lane. I wouldn't be walking up from the Fulham Road to catch it any more, near Peter's shop, because it would mean passing the end of South Bolton Gardens, where

Orpen once had his studio, and when I think of Orpen, I think of—

Well, you know who I mean.